LEGENDS OF GOSHEN SWAMP:
THE STORY OF CAPTAIN DRAKE

JAMES MILTON ROBERTS

DEDICATION

First, any dedication should go to our life-giver and Creator who without him, this book would never have happened. Psalms 83:18

Next, I want to dedicate this book, to my wife, Sandra Benson Roberts. Sandra has been a great encouragement to me during the writing by the patience she has shown, giving me space to write when she wanted my attention. She never let up on her love for me but continued to embrace me with hugs and kisses when I was discouraged.

Next, I would like to thank Webster for a fine New World College Dictionary. It has helped me greatly. Writing any kind of book is not easy. This is my second book. The first was a biography of my life and

Vietnam, it took me years to write. It was mainly for therapy for PTSD and amnesia.

Sandra, again has helped me greatly with my PTSD, and I have a service dog named Dexter. He is a fullblooded Rottweiler, fully trained, and does wonders in aiding me as a service dog.

INTRODUCTION

My name is James Milton Roberts, and this is a book based on fiction. The part about the Civil War Contents is mostly true. There are other names and places in the book that are true. You should look at the book as a book of fiction; never try to base it on fact. Jake Strader never existed; the name Strader I saw on the side of a cargo truck at an intersection. This book has been going over and over in my mind for about a year and a half, if not longer, until it was completed on February 23, 2021.

I am a disabled veteran 100% totally and permanently disabled due to a service-connected disability from Viet Nam. I have free time to spend writing, but words and thoughts do not come easily for me. My next book should not take near as long as the subject is already set in my mind; it will start where this one left off.

This book is about a man with a dream that he expects to last about eighty-five to ninety years at the most. Yet, that dream goes on for over three hundred years with no end in sight. The "generations" of the pirates' children continue to live that long, and so the story.

It starts in late 1698. Captain Jake Strader and his men are a band of very successful pirates. By 1705 they are looking for a place of refuge, to live out the rest of their lives in peace, and not to be hanged.

Captain Drake Strader dreams that his men and their women will live the rest of their lives in freedom in a refuge to themselves, till they die never to be hanged, with children and happy family lives.

Looking for such a place, they find it in a swamp in North Carolina. They live in the swamp up till the Civil War and they have eight men that are taken into the Confederate Army. Then the story centers on the battles of the Civil War and these two men's lives.

It will have stories about the battles during the war and events that took place, including names of the Generals involved in the battles, number of casualties, and total number fighting.

Events in the swamp will be about the different kinds of animals in Goshen Swamp. Goshen Swamp does exist in N.C. My father owned a farm when I was a young kid, and Goshen Swamp was at the rear of the farm. I spent a lot of time fishing in that old swamp. There are some pictures of what the swamp looks like. People today with modern machinery have been able to go into some parts of Goshen Swamp and pull out logs of cypress trees and some different hardwood.

The story of the swamp is an interesting one to tell if you like one of adventure and surprises of the unknown. There are a lot of treasure chests that are held by the 129 pirate family heads, filled with gold and silver. There is a group of runaway slaves that join the camp of the pirates and spend the rest of their lives in the camp.

There is a lot that unfolds in the story as it continues and many new characters, leading to a central family line. It is a book that is simple to read and not filled with complicated words.

CONTENTS

CAPTAIN DRAKE STRADER

Chapter 1

North Carolina

Starts out in 1698, Captain Drake Strader and his men are a band of pirates roaming the seas. Destroying and stealing gold and valuables from merchant ships, in great numbers.

Their time as pirates is running short and they know they have to find a good hiding place, to live out their lives, or hang. So the Captain goes on the search for such a place. In his search he finds a place in North Carolina.

Chapter 2

Traveling to Goshen Swampland

Captain Strader finds a hiding place inside the inlet at the Cape Fear River. There he sets up a post, with his ship the Maiden's Skull pulled inside. Searching the Cape Fear River far up the river, his scouts find a swamp they can live in to hide from civilization.

Problem is the British are in hot pursuit of them up the Cape Fear River.

Chapter 3

Settling into Goshen Swampland

It is now November 18, 1705 and they have found a place to set up a camp very deep into the swamp. The swamp is known as Goshen Swamp, and covers many counties in North Carolina. They are threaten with many wild beast, they have never seen or heard of before. They are even attacked by the one known as Sasquatch.

King William II is up set at the failure of the British to capture, Captain Drake Strader. He is afraid another failure will cost him in a political way. Ship Bounty hunters approach with a deal he can't refuse, to capture or kill Captain Drake Strader.

Chapter 4

Settling into the New Goshen Swamp Camp

After the attack by the Bounty hunters, the Captain knows he has to go deeper into the swamp. His scouts find an outstanding location for a new camp with a small water fall fed by a large fresh water spring. Again a couple of men are killed by Sasquatch.

On Friday, April 10, 1761 Captain Drake Strader, died in his sleep, from a sicknesses he had for several days.

Before he died he appointed as the new Captain, Rocca Lombardi. Most people called him Rock.

CAPTAIN ROCCA LOMBARDI

Chapter 5

The First Generation Raised in Goshen Swamp

Everyone called him Captain Rock. There was a mother bear that was killed by a big male bear and she had a cub. The scouts knew the cub would die left alone, so they brought it back to camp, till it was old enough to leave. It never Left!

On January 12, 1792 Captain Rock died at 92, appointing Jarrett Barlow as Captain of the camp.

CAPTAIN JARRETT

Chapter 6

More Generations Raised in Goshen Swamp

Twenty-nine black runaway slaves have now joined the camp of the pirates generation. One thing that Captain Drake Strader did was make sure all his men and their wives and children, got was an education. He was a well educated man knowing several languages. He saw to it all his people knew what he knew and more.

That went for the runaway slaves also, no exceptions for anyone in the camp. All the Captains made sure that rule was followed.

Chapter 7

1800s Goshen Swamp North Carolina

Cubed Browning is a runaway slave with a very good talent in art and sculptures, making his way to the world of art.

The Captain takes on the raising of bees for honey in the camp. Men are sent to honorary Colleges, to further their education. The worst thing to hit North Carolina and the camp was a hurricane on December 5, 1826. It was the worst thing to happen to the camp in 121 years.

CAPTAIN JASPER STANDISH

Chapter 8

Goshen Swamp and the Outside World

On Tuesday April 18, 1837 Captain Jarrett Barlow has died. Before he died he appointed as Captain Jasper William Standish. Jubal the leader of the slaves, and the others have saved enough money to buy their freedom.

THE CIVIL WAR MARTY AND JAY STANDISH

Chapter 9

Fighting With The Confederacy

Civil War has started, Marty and Jay, son's of Jasper Standish have been taken by the Confederate army. They are now solders in the war. Jasper takes 450 men and goes after his son's but finds out too late, that they have already gone to battle.

THE END OF THE WAR

Chapter 10

Marty Standisch Fighting till the End

A list of different major battles and what occurred during those battles. The final surrender at Appomattox, Virginia.

MARTY STANDISH WAR ENDS

Chapter 11

April 12, 1861- May 9,186

Marty Standish on his way home and the problems he encountered. Jay Standish and his brother with problems (PTSD) after the war, and how he solved them and found peace.

CAPTAIN DRAKE STRADER

CHAPTER ONE
North Carolina

The year is late 1698, and Captain Drake Strader, one of the earliest pirates from England to roam the seas, and has made quite a reputation for himself. Not only for himself but even many of his men are known by name by the King and his associates. Captain Drake Strader has become a wealthy man from the King's merchant ships. He has burned and sank sixteen or more ships a month after taking their cargo, treasures, valuables, and weapons.

Captain Drake Strader has destroyed so many merchant ships that they have put a heavy bounty on his head and that of his men. Demanding that King William II send out warships in search of him and his men to be hanged. Captain Drake is just too smart for the English, and also the Spanish and the French, to be captured in open seas. His knowledge of the currents, and where they are the strongest with the winds, is unheard of.

Captain Drake's ship, the Maiden's Skull, was much larger than most average ships but nothing compared to a British, French, or Spanish warship. His men were always looking for ways to trap a British or Spanish warship without destroying it. With a ship like that, they could control the seas anywhere they wanted to travel. They had the respect of most pirates in the Seas and lacked nothing, always helping fellow pirates in need, asking for nothing in return. That way, they were in debt to Captain Drake, though he never brought it up.

It was a beautiful sunny day with a good breeze filling the sails of the ship and it was moving at full speed when they noticed what appeared to be a Dutch merchant ship in the southern rise. Captain Drake confirmed that the ship was indeed a Dutch ship. That meant it would be an easy capture in most cases, usually not much gold, silver, or cash, just cargo and goods. Still, they didn't want to take any chances.

Merchant Ships had been known to have sharpshooters and expert swordsmen who put up quite a fight, especially if they were carrying gold and silver along with other valuables. Captain Strader was well equipped for about anything with his ninety-eight well-trained pirates. If the merchants gave them no trouble, they usually took what they needed and let them leave unharmed.

They pulled close within sounding distance, giving a warning. The merchant ship had cannon portholes, and when the Maiden's Skull pulled alongside, the merchant ship began firing. Captain Drake was not fooled for a minute. He had his men well trained for this kind of attack; many times they had faced this kind of battle. They knew when the enemy was loading their cannons, and they were prepared to fire when the merchants didn't expect it. The pirates were expert cannon shooters, hitting any target they chose, always staying calm, and never fearing death. They were always firing before the enemy could push their cannons back into their porthole, as it exploded.

The pirate sharpshooters were always firing until the ship got into position for close cannon fire, and the men boarding began climbing over the rails with swords, knives, guns, and clubs anything that was a weapon. There was a flood of men crossing with ropes, hanging from the air and trusses of the sails, proving to be a deadly attack. This had been done so many times each man knew what he was to do and when with precision.

They captured the ship and recovered the gold, silver, and valuables along with other cargo they needed, precious gems, and perfumes. The ship was burned and sank, with survivors left on rescue boats from their ship.

Captain Drake Strader once again has made his men and himself rich. The Captain will wisely put his wealth in a safe place on the ship, and the gold in the large safe he had specially made for an occasion like this.

The Captain only lost eleven men during the entire battle. With a crew of only eighty-seven men now, that would be no problem for him. If he needed more men, all he had to do was capture another ship and give the prisoners the choice. Did they want to join them or be thrown to the sharks; the decision was usually a no-brainer. Captain Drake Strader continued to spread fear throughout the seas and to the Caribbean's, back across the Carolina inlets to Philadelphia, back to England and the French seas. His great warrior pirates were a match to no one. Not even well-trained English seamen could stand man to man against these pirates.

The pirates constantly trained when they were at sea or on an island, learning new fighting tactics with new prisoners they captured, especially from different parts of the globe. Captain Drake Strader knew this would keep them ready and professional; he always trained with them, keeping the boredom in its place.

One of the great prizes captured from ships was a woman, but they were few. This was a cause of many fights and divisions among the men. If the problem continued and there was no solution, Captain Drake would throw garbage overboard, drawing sharks.

Then he would throw the woman to the sharks, taking care of the problem of jealously between the men. The men greatly resented what the Captain did and demanded that he replace the woman at the earliest date.

So Captain Drake said that the first inhabited island they came to, they could each collect a woman if they could control them on the ship and keep peace between the men and their women. If not, they would go overboard. Any sign of rebellion or mutiny they, too, would walk the plank to the sharks, ending the problem then and for a long time to come.

It wasn't long before they came upon an inhabited island in the Caribbean. Captain Drake made peace with the Chief and they did trading, spending several days. The pirates were getting to know the women, and when it came time to leave late that night the men kidnapped the women they wanted and fled to the safety of the Maiden's Skull. Not all of the men wanted the responsibility of a woman. They would share with their mate, which was very common among the pirates—they didn't live the best of lives.

It is now January 1705, and Captain Drake Strader and his men realize their time as pirates is getting short. The winter is cruel, snowy, and bitter but the men have built themselves solid homes. With a lifetime of the death penalty hanging over them, they would like to find somewhere to hide and never have to worry about being found again, living out their days in old age with their women. Their women by now have become hardcore, rum drinking, fighting, cussing, and sexually permissive women.

King William II is tired of hearing about Captain Drake Strader, and he has over five hundred of the best warships in the world. Many he is willing to send out to hunt down pirates. Pirate activity has increased greatly. Captain Stede Bonnet, Richard Worley, Captain Charles Vance, Harsh Temple, Captain Calico Jack, and Captain Black Beard himself are just a few that are harassing the King of England and the King of Spain and covering the seas of the world. A pirate is well blessed if he lives to be forty; only a few have. Black Beard lived to be thirty which is close to the lifespan for a pirate, maybe thirty-five.

Captain Drake Strader is only one of a great few that will live out his life to a full, ripe old happy age. He hears of pirates working around North Carolina and South Carolina with a lot of hiding places inside the rivers and outer banks. There they can escape the danger of warships and bounty ships.

Captain Drake Strader is a man that stands six foot, five and a half inches tall, hairy with a full beard, very muscular and strong, dark-complected, and from the Italian nation. He is very intelligent, more than the average man, with INSTINCTS, like those of a lion (king of the beasts) and full of common sense. His men have the greatest respect, regard, and trust to the fullest any decision that he makes because most times he is right, and it is best for them, not just him.

Captain Drake Strader and his men travel to the Carolinas

and up the Cape Fear River about ten to twelve miles, learning that it splits into two sections. One section going northwest is the largest and has the easiest travel for the ship for several miles. Then they have to travel by boat. The men load up on four boats to explore the river. They see several Indians, but they seem harmless and have no problem. They are just curious.

There seems to be plenty of wildlife and fish. They are surprised by the amount of dear, bear, beaver, raccoon, large birds, and large fish.

They travel for several days, coming across more Indians that are not as friendly but brave and ready for battle.

A few men are wounded by arrows and stones from slings, yet able to survive. The Indians are more afraid of the sound of the guns than the damage they do. After a couple of days or more, Captain Drake decides to go back to the ship with the wounded men. They had no more encounters with the Indians on the way back. Giving the men time to eat and rest up and heal, he takes more men and goes up what is called the Black River today, by boat to learn another escape route. He wants to learn everything about his surroundings for as many miles as he can so he can escape when the time is right.

He also goes up the small Cape Fear River to the northeast. He decides that this is the route he will use for his escape. It is small with plenty of fresh water and wildlife, which is very important. The further you go up the river, it gets larger and gives the people plenty of room to navigate through the river, without much obstruction from beaver dams, fallen trees, and rocks.

The enemy will expect them to escape using the largest body of water, which is the main Cape Fear River. That will take them several days downriver before realizing they have been fooled. Then several days coming back. Now they have to decide to take the Black River or the other Cape Fear River and maybe splitting their forces, which would be a big mistake.

Cape Fear River

Captain Drake decides to have a skeleton crew that will steer the ship up the large Cape Fear River as far as it will go. Then they will abandon ship and sink it, blocking the river. And having scouted the area beforehand, knowing the distance to the Small Cape Fear River, they would meet up with Captain Drake and the rest of the crew, which they knew about where to meet. The Captain would wait about twelve hours, and if the men were not there by then, the Captain would consider them captured or killed by the British or the Indians. The Captain would leave one of the smaller boats hidden along the bank of the river for the men at that location.

Captain Drake Strader and his men had everything planned out perfectly, as usual. Every man and woman knew what their job was and what to do if their mate got hurt or killed. They knew that North Carolina could be that home they all had hoped for— their paradise. It was better than they knew it would be, and it would prove to be a blessing come true.

Now they must go back to the things that were, hunting their prey and treasures. They decided to travel up toward Philadelphia where the colonies were doing a lot of trading in goods, and gold and silver and other products. North Carolina had mostly goods for the colonies along the coastal region.

Captain Drake tried to keep peace with the colonies in North Carolina since he was trying to establish a resting place there. He noticed English battleships cruising on the far rise of the Ocean, looking for pirate ships, mainly Captain Drake and Black Beard. Not only are there British warships but several days later his men report what they believe to be bounty ships patrolling up and down the coast about a couple of miles out. That doesn't bother Captain Drake. He and his men can destroy that kind of ship with no problem; however, there is nothing to gain, no treasure or goods to capture, only a good fight and giving away their position.

Captain Drake has his ship well hidden about twelve miles back inside the Cape Fear River, and chances are that a British warship will not venture back that far. Captain Drake has already given the Indians at the mouth of the Cape Fear River many gifts to battle anyone coming within a mile or two inside the mouth of the river, promising more if the battle is costly. Chances are the British warship will not enter but will send their smaller boats with soldiers to check out the river. Hopefully, the Indians will discourage any British from going further back, and if not, at least hold them up for a few days.

Black Beard was known for taking his ship inside the outer banks of North Carolina. He was a master at being able to navigate around the sandbars that wrecked so many ships, calling it the graveyard of the Atlantic. Yet in 1718, Black Beard's ship would be caught inside Ocracoke Island to battle the British in his final battle.

Black Beard would be said to have received five shots and around twenty cut wounds before he was beheaded as he was about to kill Maynard. They had been fighting for some time as he fought Maynard and other sailors. As he was about to kill Maynard, a sailor cut his neck, and with a second slash, he severed Black Beard's head. They said Black Beard fought like a demon in battle. He proved to be more famous after his death than while he was living. He only lived from 1688-1718.

Time was going by slowly, and Captain Drake's men were getting restless and wanted some action, even if the British were in that area. They decided to go to Philadelphia and hit a few merchant ships; the British couldn't be everywhere. He selected seventy-five of his most capable men and leaves the rest there at the Cape Fear Camp till they return. Just as they had planned it, they hit four merchant ships each loaded with gold, silver, all kinds of valuables, and rich perfumes. The merchants figured with the British warships and bounty ships around, it was a good time to ship their valuables.

Captain Drake Strader and his men were loaded down with valuables and headed back to their resting camp. As they were heading back, a British warship caught sight of them and began firing their cannons at them from a distance but falling way short. It was a race back to the Carolinas. Darkness set in, to their advantage, for it was a new moon. Captain Drake knew his way, close to the coastline like the back of his hand, even on a new moon.

It was dark as midnight on a new moon, and they cruised along without any problem, checking depth on all sides. Sandbars can be very tricky, especially at night. They make good time when they know they are safe.

The Maiden's Skull going Home

It wasn't long before they lost the British, but they knew at dawn that they would be looking in every hole for them after searching the deep seas.

Captain Drake knew this was the time for their plan of escape. They had all the treasure they could ever need or carry. Captain Drake ordered the men to make many different kinds of traps for the British, having trees cut and ready at the cut of a vine to fall across the river from both sides, so the last men coming from the Maiden's Skull will be able to get out quickly. They constructed swinging boulders falling from trees, and timbers cut so they will be swinging from trees, destroying men and boats. The British will find out what these men are made of when it comes to putting up a good fight.

This will be going on for some time farther up the river. The Captain ordered his men to build special boats, wide but shallow with high sides to hold treasures for shallow waters and strong handles all along the sides.

Captain Drake has around 162 people in all making the trip, counting the women and a few children. When the boats are ready, they are loaded with the treasures wrapped and tied tight. The bigger boats are loaded with people, water, food, gun power, and plenty of rum. They had tools and anything they would need at their new settlement for building and farming and mining. Captain Drake Strader and his men have been planning this since they arrived at Cape Fear. It was indeed a long convoy of boats, and they doubled and tripled side by side down the river when they could.

The Small Cape Fear River

The Captain has his spies watching for the British and what they are doing. The Captain has made friends with the Indians at the mouth of the Cape Fear River by trading goods with them. So they are used to delay the British when they start up the mouth of the Cape Fear River when he sees that the British warship will be there soon.

He gave the Indian Chief many extra gifts for himself and his warriors to attack the British for at least two days and longer if possible. Captain Drake learned the Indian language as soon as he arrived in North Carolina; he is very clever and knows several languages. Captain Strader then decides to send his ship, the Maiden's Skull, up the northwest Big Cape Fear River several miles, sinking the ship to block the river. He does hate to sink the Maiden's Skull, but it has to be done for their final escape and to fool the British. Then his men should be able to come back by boat and come up the Little Cape Fear River, waiting for the British to figure out what Captain Drake Strader has done.

This will have taken them a good two weeks or longer as the four men continue to make traps of all kinds to throw the British off their game and get them disarrayed to the point they didn't know what was up or down. These pirates were well skilled at making traps for the British going and coming up the Cape Fear River. Joe Jo was with them and he was a master trapper of animals of all sizes. The British boats were a new challenge, but he was excited to accept it.

When the British finally arrive, they set up camp before setting out at daylight. Setting off the traps as the British make their way up the river, they are caught completely by surprise and confusion. When the British finally figure out what Captain Drake has done, it has caused so much damage and death to the British soldiers and seamen, by only four men, and cost a lot of time. This seems to go on and on with no end.

Finally, the four men leave with no harm to themselves, catching up with the party, many days down the river instead of crossing the swamps as they planned earlier. If the Indians were not helping to hold back the British, it would not have worked.

Everything was going as planned, and Captain Drake wanted to stay on the Little Cape Fear River as long as he could. Then he wanted to find an uninhabited swampland area and go as deep into the swamp as he could to find a suitable living spot. He would then send out eight scouts in different directions in search of the perfect home site. The trip would be hard, hot and cold, and sometimes freezing.

It was now around early August 1705. Summer was about over, and it was rainy with at least one thunderstorm every afternoon. Staying on the river made it much cooler for everyone, and work was easier. The fifty or sixty miles or more was not so bad; it took a little more than four weeks. From there they encountered more fallen trees, beaver dams, and large rocks. Some large ponds had developed and made good resting places with good hunting areas. This is where the four British troublemakers caught up with the Captain and the crew.

Captain Drake always had scouts on the lookout as far back as where the British were. He was always well informed with scouts in pairs to the north, east, west, and south. Captain Drake did send four scouts to go long- range on foot along the bank of the Little Cape Fear River making notes, but it was only on their way back that they wrote a report of blockage, beaver dams, settlers, Indian camps, rapids, pools, and good hunting grounds.

They were to go till they thought they found a good crossing that would lead to a good swampland area.

Then and only then would they report back after finding the swampland. They didn't have to scout the swampland, just find some that was far away and out of the way of human habitation. Being in pairs, one would go back when something important needed to be reported, while the other continued onward. If settlers lived along the River, Captain Drake knew it. If Indians camped along the river, he knew it. They had to wait till late nightfall to pass on the river. Their procession was so long it would take two nights for them to pass. Captain Drake Strader would stay behind with the last boat after getting word from his scouts that everything was OK. This made them feel secure, knowing who was near them. When they were safe, he would go back up front to make further decisions. The others would keep traveling, clearing the way for them, and it wouldn't be long before they would catch up.

It was too risky to let anyone know who they were and where they were going. Their freedom for the rest of their lives depended upon secrecy.

At that time, they didn't know it but they were headed very deep, several miles, into Goshen Swamp in Duplin County, North Carolina, to the refuge they had hoped for. It would be hard, wet, rugged, and full of varmints of all sizes—I mean SIZES.

CAPTAIN DRAKE STRADER

CHAPTER TWO
Traveling to Goshen Swampland

Turns out the four men have returned and have good news. One of them stopped at a trading post in Beautancus, North Carolina, and found out that Goshen Swamp was not far from there. A tradesman gave him the directions to Goshen Swamp and he met with the other three men waiting for him under the weeping willow tree. They made their way to Goshen Swamp and were very excited at what they saw. They got started right away, traveling day and night to meet Captain Drake.

It was urgent that they get back as quickly as possible.

On the way back they did come across a hunting party of six Indians, so they had to lay low in a gully covered with fallen trees. They stayed about two and a half hours to make sure that the Indians were gone. The Indians would keep circling back, trying to surprise a deer they were watching. They also had their eye on a bald eagle that kept circling, watching a fox. If the eagle came down to try and carry off the fox, he may not be able to lift off with it. That would give the Indians a good chance to kill or capture the eagle and the fox. Eagle feathers are important to the Indians and have a spiritual connection to the spirit life for them. As the Indians are occupied with the fox, eagle, and deer, the four pirates make their way down the river. It is not long until they are on their way to meet the Captain. They are making notes as they go, and it is not long before they are at the camp.

When they report what they have found to Captain Drake Strader, he is more than excited. It sounds just like what they are looking for. He calls in his scouts and his chief advisers and fills everyone in on what he has been told. Then they start making their plans in every detail, from the time they leave the camp at the pond till they reach the swampland.

This includes going past the settlements they know about and a small Indian camp and clearing out beaver dams and trees in the way. There are no rapids or rock formations of any size that will be a problem.

After making their plans and all the key men and key women knew what was expected of them in detail, the Captain then went out to all 162 people and explained what was going on and what they were going to do, starting at daylight the next morning. He also reminded them that the British were still coming up the Cape Fear River, but slowly. The British were expecting attacks as they traveled, so they moved slowly and cautiously. The scouts were still setting up traps for them. These guerrilla tactics were very effective, causing damage, injury, and death to the British, but not one pirate had any injuries. This again went back to their fighting skills and instincts for battle.

The British found themselves having to stop and repair boats constantly while building rafts or makeshift boats in order to continue, all because of four skilled men working a lot at night and using some gun power. The British don't know if they are dealing with six men, or if there could be two dozen men.

Captain Drake and his people are on the move before sunrise. Everyone is excited and looking forward to the trip, no matter how tough. This is the freedom and peace they have looked forward to for so long. When they get into the swamp, they will lose the British for good, or get rid of them one way or the other. When the British started, there were around 265 sailors and soldiers. The British Captain, Winslow Mansfield, is determined to capture or destroy Captain Drake Strader and his cutthroat men. The British were dying fast from yellow fever, a touch of malaria and dysentery, and from the four pirates also.

Captain Drake Strader and his men had a remedy for the fever that the Indians gave him, that helped hold down the fever and other fevers. The herb was found in the swamp from the root of a bush, it was not a cure but almost.

The Captain had no losses from the fever but did have a lot of men laid up and working when they could. These men were dedicated and knew that when their fever broke, the danger was past. They then got up and went back to work knowing how important each man was.

It would not be long before the British would be headed their way. They wanted to make sure they were well ahead of them so that they would not have to make a stand and fight.

They made time very fast once they were going. Scouts with men went ahead and blew up and destroyed beaver dams in the way as well as trees crossing the river. This way the crew continued to move at a steady speed. Very seldom did they have to stop, only for settlements and the Indian camps was all, but it didn't take as long as usual. The convoy was able to move very rapidly from then on and meet the scouts at their destinations by mid- afternoon. It was a good start, unloading on dry land and knowing they were that much closer to their new homeland.

Captain Drake Strader told the men to start making wagon wheels and axles to fit under the boats. This would carry them over land and they again could use the boats in the swamps. There were a lot of pins, clamps, and vices used in the work of building the wooden wheels and fitting them under the boats. They still had to worry about the British, keeping an eye on them constantly and realizing they would be getting too close soon.

Time was a very important factor at this point. The men hurried, working day and night as they were skilled laborers. They worked in shifts and relieved men from their duties when it was obvious they were too tired to continue. These men were tough, determined, dedicated, and hard to the core, unstoppable.

The men wanted a fight with the British, but Captain Drake knew it was not the time. It would happen only if necessary because he wanted every man to taste freedom in Goshen Swampland and not one to die in a fight with the British unnecessarily. It was too close for them to start taking chances or gambling. It would only be a couple of days longer and they would be on the move.

Scouts had been reporting back about when and where was the best time to move at day or at night and the hours that would be best. Captain Drake's scouts were very effective and accurate about their decisions. Everything was falling into place perfectly. Other scouts went deep into Goshen Swampland looking for a temporary place for them to settle. It didn't have to be perfect, just comfortable for the time being, and somewhere they could lose Captain Winslow Mansfield of the British Navy and reorganize. They had to be there long enough till they found what they were wanting and keep them through the winter.

Captain Drake finally got everything organized to move out at first light the next morning. It was now September 1, 1705. Autumn would begin in twenty-three days, and winter will start December 21. Hopefully, it will be a mild winter, and if not, Captain Drake has planned ahead with dried meat to help them through. It is nothing great, but for surviving, it will work if used sparingly.

September to December should give them time to build strong houses that are windproof and rainproof. The swamp should give them plenty of good fishing and hunting for food and clothing and storage for winter. There will be plenty of areas to do both, with a lot of firewood nearby.

The next day they start to move out in their long wagon train. Everyone says it feels good to be on land. Captain Drake left behind several men to finish sweeping down the area where they camped. hen the scouts would report to these men when the British were coming and how much time they had. They would cut large brush to plant along the shoreline while it is still green to hide the place where the pirates came ashore. If this worked, they would go up the Cape Fear River for miles before realizing they had been fooled. Then when they came back down the Cape Fear River, they would see the wilted brush and know what the pirates did. It was critical that they fooled the British. It would mean a battle with the British at the entrance of Goshen Swamp or not, because of the shortage of time. If the British were fooled and they went by, they would be gone for weeks, but if not, real trouble and a big battle.

The scouts waited around for hours, and finally the British were seen coming up the river slow and cautiously as if looking for a fight. The scouts hid in the thick brush and up in the large trees that were hundreds of years old. They were watching every move the British were making. They were clenching and biting their fists as they watched the British sail by in their boats with their small sails attached. Finally, they were clear, and the pirates wanted to wait through the night till daylight, to make sure the British had taken the fool's trap for sure. The British should be gone now for many days if not for weeks, giving the pirates all the time they need, without being rushed.

With the scouts convinced that Captain Winslow Mansfield of the British Navy had moved up the Cape Fear River, they decided to move on and join the rest of the crew.

By sunrise they were all ready, had breakfast and coffee, and were on the move. They traveled slowly cautiously until they came to the trading post at Beautancus. There they had one of the men get new supplies and a little fresh gun power, tobacco, and bacon and then make his way back to the other three men.

They were waiting under an old weeping willow tree, the most humble tree in the forest. They now took time out to eat a good meal of aged smoked cured ham, beans, bread, and some thick country gravy the keeper had on the stove. After eating they were so full, laying under that tree with the wind blowing a good strong breeze, they went to sleep and slept for two hours of needed rest.

Waking up rested about mid-afternoon they started out and headed toward Goshen Swamp to meet up with the others in the group who were in a hurry to get moving.

Weeping Willow

Captain Drake Strader and the group were having problems. Some wheels were coming off regularly because of not having proper nuts to screw them on. They had to use leather straps to tie around the axles' ends. Then there were a few axles that were cut from Red Oak instead of Cypress or White Oak, and they broke after they had some wear and tear. Captain Drake still made the convoy continue forward as he would continue to lead the group. The others would catch up when they stopped to camp for the night. If anyone didn't make it by morning, eight to twelve men were sent back to find them and give any needed assistance.

It looked as if they may make it by the next day around the

mid-afternoon with the problems they were having. Captain Drake was still getting steady reports from his scouts. There were always problems, but the Captain was a problem solver and had the solution. Captain Drake had one scout he was especially fond of; they called him Joe Jo. Joe Jo was from a very large jungle island in the Pacific that the pirates took captive. He was a skilled scout, tracker, and trapper.

He was one of the four pirates that gave the British so much trouble. Joe Jo was bad news for anyone he was against. The only way the Captain's men caught him was that he was taking an afternoon nap as they were slithering up on him. He could track anything in the jungle whether it be animal, man, or beast, no matter what. Joe Jo had taught the other scouts most of what he knew, and they taught him about traveling by the stars and the currents in the seas. Joe Jo was a medium-sized man, and he was very witty, clever, and happy as they come. The next morning they took a headcount and almost everyone was present. Those that had trouble and were lagging behind came straggling in during the night. Others in the camp saved leftover food for the lagers when they came in, knowing they would be exhausted and ready for bed. The next morning they got started about an hour after sunrise, everyone double-checked their equipment and reinforced what they could.

They had several water buffalo's to help pull the boats along with a few milk cows. They were so strong they could pull more than one, sometimes three, depending on the weight. The water does not bother the water buffalo at all; they like the water as well as the land. They make good farming animals, too. The pirates don't plan to do much farming, but if they do find a big enough clearing, some may give it a try. They will need fresh vegetables, to keep them healthy and a little tobacco for smoking and chewing. They don't want to forget the corn and sugar cane for their moonshine, so they will do quite a bit of farming after all.

They are moving along very steadily, making good time. They only have six small children and one mother expecting. They are four boys and two girls. The oldest boy is named Orsin; they call him Bear. The next is Luka Barlow; he is always active and moving. Then there is Rocca Lombardi whom they call Rock because that is the meaning of his name in Italian.

Captain Drake likes that because he is Italian. Then there is Bruno who is the youngest of the four but maybe the stoutest and strongest. The oldest girl's name is Tessa and the youngest is Sarah. These six were all born on the Maiden's Skull around the year 1700 or a little later, so they were all around four to six years old and tough as their parents. For kids, you couldn't ask for any better under these conditions, never crying or complaining.

These kids had plenty of moms and dads taking care of them.

The Captain was making good time going across the flat land but then one of the boats' axles broke. They were not that far from the swampland, so they sent out scouts to find a good cypress for the axle. While they were gone Captain Drake sent some men out to find a good size white oak branch to be shaved down for the axle, too. The men found a good strong white oak branch and started shaving it down. When the other men got back with the cypress pole, they sized it up and cut it to fit for another axle that broke, saving them much time. Time goes on and the wheels start coming off. Captain Drake decides to take a break and have all the wheels redone and reinforced, knowing it will save time in the long run. Everything is finished, and they are on the move again. It is getting close to mid-afternoon, and they are nearing the Goshen Swamp entrance. Everyone now is getting anxious and excited and beginning to move faster.

One of the scouts comes back and says the entrance is about a mile ahead. As it would be, a boat axle breaks. Everyone keeps going while the one with the broken axle gets it repaired in no time with the cypress pole that was just fixed earlier. Finally, everyone is introduced to Goshen Swampland on November 12, 1705.

They make their camp for the night and the next day take the needed rest. Captain Drake Strader sends out scouts to go as far as the British, to learn their exact location. They are to remove the axles and wheels, burn them, and then bury them along with anything else that can't be carried. They must still hide their trail, especially to the entrance into Goshen Swampland. The soil here is solid with sand mixed and steady in the woody areas. It has been raining almost every evening. The swamp is running a little high with water, which will make it easier with the boats when they get to the main run in the swamp.

Once they get into the main run of the swamp, they can go deeper into the swamp for as many miles as they would like. This is where their scouts will have proved their value because the swamp continues to split in many directions. Some go on a short distance to a dead end while others circle back to the beginning. Then there are ones that go a long distance, ending up at larger rivers with no results. This gave Captain Drake a better selection for all the needs of the camp.

Goshen Swamp Entrance

Captain Drake Strader decides to wait till they are into the swamp and going down the main run before he takes a look at the split-offs the scouts will recommend. All the scouts have looked at the splits and settled on three. The Captain will select what he considers the best for all the needs of the camp.

Late the next morning the scouts report back to Captain Strader to tell him that Captain Winslow Mansfield of the British Navy, found their cut-off route at the Cape Fear River that morning. They appeared to be setting up camp for a few days, where the pirates had themselves earlier set up camp.

The Main Run

Captain Drake then said that Captain Winslow had sentscouts back to see if they had missed anything and found the dying bushes. That was how he was able to get back so quickly. Now he had to make a change of plans. They knew that there was going to be a night battle about 3:00 a.m. with a lot of explosives and knife attacks while men slept.

Captain Drake got the pirates together, around ninety-eight of them, and they made their plans with precision as usual. They wanted to destroy the boats, cannons, and the supply and weapons depot with explosives when they were discovered. They had a crew for that. Before that time, men would be going from bedroll to bedroll, cutting throats and stabbing as many men as possible.

Everything went off better than expected, and Captain Winslow Mansfield lost three-fourths of his men while the rest were wounded or sick with fever.

He only had a skeleton crew left with few supplies and had to repair or build boats to get back to his ship.

Maybe he could get one boat stable enough to go back to the mother ship and get some help?

He had to give up his quest to capture Captain Drake Strader for quite a while. At least until he would meet another British battleship and could restock with men and supplies since it was the King's wish to capture Captain Drake Strader, especially since Captain Winslow Mansfield knew exactly where he was.

One thing was for sure, Captain Mansfield was a very determined man and had set his mind to return. Captain Drake won another battle with no fatal injuries, and his men made their way back to Goshen Swamp. The men celebrated over the fight that they had been quarreling about for weeks.

CAPTAIN DRAKE STRADER

CHAPTER THREE
Settling into Goshen Swampland

It was on November 18, 1705, when Captain Drake Strader and his 156 pirates and 6 children set out into the dreaded Goshen Swampland, full of all kinds of insects, snakes, beasts, bears, wild cats, and animals that they had never seen. Animals you never see during the day but catch only a silhouette of at night, hear from a distance, and sometimes find close to your bedroll with a vicious growl and drooling. Everyone was in great hope, excitement, and fear. This was a great adventure. This was going to be slow-moving as Captain Drake and the three scouts were going to look at the three locations they had picked out.

They had a few canoes burned out especially for this trip. They were gone for a couple of days, but they had what they thought to be the best locations. This would get them through the winter, and it had a small clearing for vegetables. Everyone would have room to build their houses strong and steady, keeping out wind and rain.

They were deep enough into the swamp that they would be hard to find. There were so many twists and turns that the pirates would know when anyone was coming days before they even got close. They could do battle with anyone long before they found their camp. Goshen Swamp was just full of what they had always wanted: plenty of food, fish, dear, fox, coon, wild hogs, and lots of large birds. Freshwater was a problem; there was not a large supply. It had to be stored in barrels when it rained from the run-off of the houses and other sources they had prepared.

Everyone moved into their locations without a lot of major problems it was very disorganized at first. People had to make do with what they had. Others tried to give a little extra help to the ones with kids. The women that were pregnant were getting along better than most women. They didn't try to do too much the first evening they were in but mostly tried to get used to the area and discover what they could make use of.

They did get up early the next morning and started organizing everything. After that they started building homes. The first were the homes for the families with children and pregnant women. Everyone got together, and the seven houses were completed before sunset.

There were a lot of trees around and a lot of mud to fill the cracks in the walls. Chimneys had to be built using cypress wood since there were very few stones around.

With the few stones there were, they made a community oven and grill. For the first time in a long time, the men and women had oven-baked bread and barbecued meat, for a get-together. It was good for everyone to finally be able to settle down, be comfortable, and enjoy a good meal and rest. They were excited to be at their home base for at least some time to celebrate.

They did have to get an early start the next morning because they had more houses to build. Everyone would have the same basic house with no extras, just something to keep the cold, rain, and wind out. It would be dry, to make bedroll on the floor and build a fire in the chimney. Later they would build a bed and table with chairs; that's all one needs besides maybe a storage box for some clothes or other items.

Everyone was organized and ready, so they started out in their selected groups. They had a group that was building many water barrels because they were running so short. This would keep them from having to travel deeper into the swamp to get fresh water from a couple of springs they found. There was plenty of water in the swamp but it was stagnated and bad and would give you the fever.

Everyone was as busy as bees trying to build houses, water barrels, and drainage ditches to dry out the camp area. This was a large task because it entailed going to a lower spot to move the water down below their area. It was hard, but it was working. The water buffalo were a great help in making the trench that drain the water from the campsite.

Finally, after about two weeks, things were coming together; they weren't done, but you could see the end. Only a few more homes to build and the area was finally dry. Joe Jo and a couple more scouts had gone out to search for food hoping to kill a deer, wild hog, or something that would make a large meal. They saw a herd of about twelve deer on a grassy knoll, so they shot two of them. Later they saw a large flock of around eighteen turkeys, killing four. Joe Jo killed two with one shot; they were standing side by side.

They had to build a special frame for the boat to carry the meat home. When they got home the other scouts also had killed some meat, and they were cooking it on the community oven and grill. Joe Jo decided they would get a little to eat, then they would dress out the deer and the turkeys. After everyone ate they all went to bed with a couple of guards keeping watch from the trees.

These pirates could never have believed that they would have this freedom and this good of a time if they were not living it. It was all thanks to Captain

Drake Strader for coming up with the ingenious idea.

By this time it was about the end of January 1706.

Winter had come fast, and there was a lot of firewood to be cut for everyone. It had to last the entire winter no one wanted to cut wood in the snow or freezing rain. They had to hunt for more meat to store because no one wants to hunt in the snow and freezing rain, either. A lot still had to be made ready for winter.

Yes, everyone was going to bed, ready to get a good night's sleep and get up early. Excitement would wake them tomorrow, giving them new things to worry about. They left food on the community oven and grill.

Sometime during the early morning, when the guards had dozed off, a large beast came into the camp and tore up the grill, taking the meat, growling, snorting, scratching, and trying to destroy anything that got in its way. It broke the gate open on both sides of the gateway. The guards were so shocked and shook up, one fell out of the tree while the others' rifle fell out of the tree and went off.

Everyone came outside scared to death, wanting to know what had happened. No one had seen anything, the guards were asleep, and when they came to their senses, they were trying to stay in the tree or get off the ground. Captain Drake said they would send out a search party at daylight and repair the grill and gate then, too. Everyone was to go back to bed and try to get some rest.

The morning sun came up with a chill in the air, and Captain Drake looked over the damage that was done. He said that whatever it was, it was big, mean, dangerous, and very, very strong. It was no average beast that destroyed their camp this morning. There were drool and foam all over the grill where the monster ate the leftovers. He wasted no time, he must have taken some meat with him when he left.

Captain Drake took eight men with him to track the beast in case they had to slip up on it and try to capture it. The beast left in such a rush that he left broken brush for a long distance. Then he drifted off into the water, and the men had to spread out. It was as if he had vanished; he was gone with no sign of him anywhere and no sign that he came out of the water or that he could have continued in the water. Whatever it was, it knew its way around the swamp, and it was almost impossible to track. Now and then they would find a large footprint, then a speck of stiff hair on a thorn bush and that would be about it.

The Captain decided that by the time they got back to Camp, it would be close to dark. They had never gone that far into the swamp in that direction before. So they started making their way back, trying to remember landmarks, and yet so many look the same. These men do have good memories and a sense of direction. They make it back to camp before dark and just in time for supper.

While they were gone, the remaining men had pulled off most of the other chores and repaired the grill and the gate this time making them stronger and steadier.

Captain Strader realized that the brush border they had used before was not going to be strong enough to keep out vicious animals. So he had selected several men to start building poles pointing up beside each other, like a fort, with a catwalk. This would keep out wild animals and be good for fighting off intruders that may slip by. Winter has set in and everyone is well stocked with food, meat, clothing, and firewood. They are still short of fresh water and vegetables. The deeper into winter they get, the colder it gets, and people get sicker. The settlement is clean and thriving, the people get along very well because this is their refuge, their place of peace.

The men still go out and hunt and fish in the winter with

success, bringing home prize catches. Surprising as it may be, the people are doing very well with the cold winter, ice, and snow. The freshwater would have to be brought in from outside, it would be frozen and need to be thawed out to be used. About a week out of the year, it would get so cold the swamp would freeze over about one to two inches. That would make it hard to get fresh water, so they would wait till the ice melted.

As winter passed, work began to progress more quickly. The fortified walls were almost complete, and by bringing the food inside, it meant that the animals and the beast would stay outside. They didn't have any more problems with the beast, but they did hear noises and movements outside the camp, and the guards were sure it was the beast coming back for more food. The Captain did give strict orders that no food of any kind would be left outside in the future.

Captain Drake Strader decides the camp needs to go to the trading post at Beautancus and get needed supplies. He will send four men and three women, all dressed as people of the land as best they can. They don't want to look like pirates!

Turns out that while they are there, they are watching trappers skin and cure their catches. So they question them about how to trap. They buy several traps and bring them back to the camp with them. Captain Drake likes the idea of the traps, and they set them out by the run of the swamp. Joe Jo is able to show the best places to hide the traps to get the best results. The next day, when they came back to check their traps, they are all triggered.

They have caught many different kinds of animals: fox, raccoon, beaver, weasel, and others. They were able to skin and dry the furs for use, sale, or trade. This venture was proving more encouraging than expected.

There were a lot of furs and hides from the different animals, especially deer and some bears. That was good trading at the trading post for needed medicine and supplies. The new supplies really picked up the spirits of the people in the camp. Everyone was so excited and full of life with new clothing they had made from the new cloth and new boots some of the men had.

The walls for the fort were up now, and the guards didn't have to sleep in the trees any longer. Now they had a catwalk to walk on that would keep them busy and awake. The Captain could also look out his window at any time to check on them; so could the others. If anyone was caught sleeping, he was given the duty of cutting extra firewood for the winter. No one wanted that job, especially by themselves.

The men, on their hunting trips and scouting explorations for better living sites, have been coming across some very special sightings and a few, exciting experiences. Joe Jo had a run-in with a very large hairy beast that stood around nine to ten feet tall, stealing a badger he had trapped in one of his traps. He slapped the badger one time with his right hand, killed it, and tore it from the trap with ease. Then it walked off. Joe Jo said without question this was what tore up their camp and was what folks from the past had called Sasquatch. He was described as being just like what the others had seen.

A couple of other men had seen a Sasquatch leap from behind a cypress tree, attack a large buck deer taking a drink of water from the swamp, snap its neck like a twig, then carry it off like it was a small fox. The men said they had never seen such strength in anything; even a large bull could not stand against this beast. This beast was broad and hairy, had a large head, with large teeth and sharp dreadful eyes. His arms slung down low on his body as he walked straight with a slumped shoulder. The only problem was they were so far away they could not really get as good a look at him as they wanted. They gave only a description of what it looked like.

It was good that Captain Drake Strader had built the camp as well as he did, but could it keep out a Sasquatch? That question remained to be seen! It looked like they may have to spend another winter here, so the Captain decided to build a blockhouse at each corner so the guards could come in out of the weather and still keep guard. The Captain even had their cannons in place along the walls and in the yard. They could then take care of any head-on attack they would face.

It was planting season, and many of the families were planting gardens next to their homes. This would give them the vegetables that they need. Dredging the water off to the lower section of the swamp helped make more dry land for planting. Some of the women had been planting wildflowers they had come across in the swamp, making the camp look more like home. This also brought many different species of birds and other little critters, squirrels, rabbits, and skunks.

The woman that was pregnant had her baby in the winter, and it was a healthy girl. Now two other women were expecting, one around September and the other around November. It was around May 12, 1706, and time had moved fast. They had gotten a lot done in that amount of time. They had lived healthy, and for the most part, lived very well.

Now it was time to search more seriously for a permanent home that would last from then on. That meant till they died or got amnesty and decided to leave. They knew there was nothing for them on the outside; others who got amnesty ended up getting hanged anyway or going to prison. They could never adjust to life with people on the outside; they were too different in their ways.

Captain Drake Strader decided to send out more scouts with more supplies and water, sending them deeper into the swamp with traps for food so they could do long-range scouting for months if necessary. The Captain didn't want them coming back without results. Joe Jo was to be in charge, and everyone would report back to him weekly, or longer, as he chose. Then they would go out again setting a new destination to meet at until they had success.

The men would continue building boats that would float through the swamp when they were ready to move to the new location. These boats had to be specially made to fit the condition of the swamp with a load. It would take many.

At night, the guards were reporting the sounds of what they thought were large bears fighting in the swamp. They would run through the brush and struggle with one another and then run through the swamp and be gone. They had managed to trade for two large iron pots for washing clothes in, and the women were busy doing laundry today for the camp. They also had a sewing circle going, making clothes from skins and some cloth they had traded for.

One of the scouts that were stationed at the entrance of Goshen Swamp came to report to the Captain that there were British soldiers at the entrance of Goshen Swamp. This meant that it would not be long before they would be coming down the swamp toward the camp. Would they be deep enough into the swamp to discourage them from going any further?

The Entrance To Goshen Swamp

Great fear fell over everyone in the camp, for they felt that they had not gone deep enough into the swamp. Captain Drake said not to worry; there were too many outlets, and it was not likely they would pick the right ones. They would keep an eye on them, and if they reached a certain location, they would set up an ambush and keep hitting them after that.

Different outlets the British had to choose from

The British set up their camp at the entrance and then sent scouts into the swamp. They returned days later, without any good results. They finally decided to enter the swamp, moving slowly, taking the route the scouts had selected. After days of fighting extra-large snakes, spiders, lizards, mosquitoes, fleas, vines, poison ivy, thorny briers, and attack by wild cats, bears, and even a few gators, these homely British were ready to go home. But their captain was not about to give up at this point.

Turns out they had spent almost three months in the swamp and were getting very close to the ambush point. Then the captain of the British Forces decided that the pirates had fallen fate to the swamp and fever, existing no more. Then he told his men they would try to find their way out as best they could. When they finally found their way out, they had suffered great losses due to fever, snake bite, animal attack, drowning, and other unforeseen occurrences.

They went home, making a full report of their ordeal and their casualties, their men saying they would never go through anything like that again. The captain was approached by bounty hunters and asked for a copy of his report, a description of his trip through the swamp, and how far he went.

Captain Drake Strader is sitting outside his house in the evening, he is restless, thinking about the British leaving. He can't sleep, just listening to the swamp sounds and wondering what they are, where they are, and how many. He hears wild cats just outside the camp, wondering if they are mating cries or battle cries. Then there was a lot of threshing in the swamp nearby, like an animal being attacked.

Captain Drake leaned back against his house and suddenly noticed a cottonmouth between his leg and the small fire he had burning.

He quickly grabbed a stick of wood and smashed the snake's head. Never dropping his pipe from his mouth. He threw the water moccasin to the side, sitting back down to watch a raccoon play with some skins they had drying. He watched the full moon shine across the yard of the camp and the guards carefully walking back and forth as they watched through the swamp for any unusual movement that may bring alarm.

Captain Strader was very excited about his people's accomplishments. The thing that is keeping him awake is that the British searched every vein and channel in that swamp up to where they stopped.

They also made a report when they got back, so someday, if someone wants to pick up where they left off, they will find them if they stay where they are at. So if they do stay, they will have to reinforce their entrance of attack sooner than before, making it stronger.

The next morning, before sunrise, Captain Strader set the alarm to get everyone up and tell them his plan. The women were fixing breakfast and making meals for the men. When the men got ready they started out to a good location, setting up the traps. Everyone said now would be a good time to have Joe Jo, but he taught us well. Every kind of trap you could think of was being set at different distances. Traps to kill, lame, and destroy both boats and supplies.

These were set all the way up to the camp, then they had the camp reinforced with walls and cannons, plenty of food, and freshwater. After six weeks of hard work, it was finally completed.

Everyone went back to doing what they were doing before, and the mosquitoes were driving everyone crazy. Everyone except Old Morgan; he was never bothered by mosquitoes. His friends would go to visit him just to get away from the mosquitoes. The people ask Captain Drake to go and talk with Morgan to find out why he was not bothered by mosquitoes. So Captain Drake went to ask Old Morgan, why?

Captain Strader approached Mr. Morgan's house, and going in, he right away noticed no mosquitoes. After a warm invitation, they had a few drinks of rum and told some wild stories. Then the Captain got to the point and said why he was there.

Morgan said that he was drinking rum one night while soaking his feet in salt water. He was using the root treatment that the Indians gave them for a slight fever when he staggered over and fell over the table, spilling the rum and the salt water that was mixed for his feet and the root treatment. He and his wife collected all they could and saved it for some reason. Then they cleaned up the mess the best they could. The next day they noticed that there were no mosquitoes in or around the house. It remained that way for over two weeks.

The Captain asked Morgan if he would give him the remainder of the mix. He took the mix, and based on what Morgan had told him, he started an experimental test, trying to find the right combination that would work. It didn't take long based on what he was told. With trial and error, he finally came up with the solution that Morgan had exactly. Then he mixed up a large amount to spread around the camp and in the homes. The men did just as they were ordered, spreading it all around the camp, in the homes, and around the outside of the camp where they traveled the most when doing duties. This worked for three months.

Mr. Morgan asked Captain Drake Strader if he would write up a contract for him, giving him the right to own the formula for the insect repellent. This would give him protection if he was able to go back to the free world and get a copyright. The Captain gladly wrote him the document, signing, dating, and doing the notary with his seal, as Captain.

The summer had come to an end, and there was still no word from Joe Jo and the scouts. It was a good summer and the gardens produced well with the rich soil. There was plenty of firewood and meat in the smokehouse.

A few weeks went by, and on September 30, 1706, Joe Jo and the scouts returned not only safely but with a treasure-load of furs and skins to be prepared for market. They had also found the resting place, the "paradise," everyone was looking for. They had many stories to tell, about exciting places they had come across and the freshwater, all they would need, to cook, wash clothes, and bathe every day.

They told about finding a warm pool of water. It had gators in it, and you had to be very careful when in the pool. There were only about six or eight of them, and they were very mean. The men spoke about run-ins with Sasquatch, bears, and other strange beasts. The swamp was no place to travel alone or far from camp unless you were scouting with two or three others.

Captain Drake decided to wait until mid-Spring before making the trip to their new location. They had already built over half the boats they would need to carry them and their cargo to their new home. This would give the scouts time to recover from their long trip. Also, the rest of the people would be busy preparing for the journey, without having to be in a hurry.

The winter goes by; it's not too bad of a winter. Everyone is doing well, the two women that were expecting had their children. They both had two healthy boys; seems the swamp is good for childbirth and raising kids. The kids find plenty of work to do and have time for their schooling. Captain Drake teaches some of the classes, teaching them other languages. They, being young, may someday decide to go into the free world. They are not under any kind of charge against the Crown or any law. The children are mischievous and find plenty to do around the camp, keeping their parents busy.

The Spring of 1707 has come, and with it brings a new problem. Bounty ships have gotten copies of the last British report from their entry into Goshen Swamp. King William II wants to avenge the failure of his last two attempts to capture Captain Drake Strader and his band of pirates.

The bounty hunters have approached King William II party members with a plan, but they will need money and men. The King decides to supply the men with what they need as far as money. They can afford the men they need and supplies. The King figures that if they fail, it won't look bad on him, but if they have success, he will look very good.

It was sunrise and the guard from the entrance to the swamp came rushing in, saying men were gathered at the entrance. A large force ready for battle with boats fit for the swamp. They were set and prepared as if they knew what they were doing. The Captain told everyone not to worry. They all knew just what to do. Get ready to go to their places when told.

Be ready as planned and wait for the enemy, then do what they are trained to do. They have nothing to fear, they have done this many times, just on ships. Now they have more to fight for; they have found their new home, and this will be their last fight, hopefully.

Everyone made their way to their station, it may be a long wait, maybe days. Before they left they took supplies and plenty of water. This could be a long wait, so the Captain decided to send out scouts to keep an eye on the intruders letting them get closer before sending out the men.

The bounty hunters did know where they were going and didn't spend a lot of time going down the wrong split of the run in the swamp. They were well prepared and organized, not going down useless splits and outlets. They had studied the British notes and maps well.

After a few weeks, the Captain told everyone to go ahead and take their station and stay alert and smart. Then it happened. Here they came, two boats wide, as expected. They let them pass for a while till better than a third had passed.

First Ambush Spot

Then they open fire while cutting down trees to block the other boats. Timbers swing across, crashing into boats killing men, and destroying boats all over the place. This was causing so much panic that the enemy as a fighting force was useless and completely caught off guard. The only survivors were wounded so badly they had to support each other to live. They had to sit in a boat in the rear because no one knew the way back without the map; they were helpless. The captain of the bounty ship had the map, and he was not about to give it up to anyone. The captain had a shoulder wound, but he was not about to slow down. He was more angry and agitated with the fact that he headed into the trap unprepared.

Captain Drake's men moved to their next position and got ready. The bounty hunters waited till the next day. They came again, but this time they were ready. They were behind cover and with their rifles at the ready. Their boats were two by two but staggered and not side by side. The pirates let them go by as usual, then again they cut the trees to stop the other boats. Captain Drake's men did the same but without as much damage. The men in the other boats managed to make their way to the front to help, so they had to pull out early. They still did a large amount of damage to the boats and their supplies.

The enemy was quick to reinforce and get on the move again. This was the Captain's last stand before the camp. They had to stop them this time. Everyone was in position again, and this time every shot must count, and every man must count. They didn't have enough time to get ready like before, but they were prepared beforehand. It didn't take the bounty hunters long, and they were fighting mad and ready to kill. This time for sure, they would not be caught by surprise again.

Second Ambush Spot

Here they come, just like before, they were all moving down the swamp in the same formation. They were not surprised when the Captain fired the first shot. Everything went as planned, but they didn't destroy the enemy, and there was a force left. They had to retreat to the camp and prepare to defend it with all they had.

Third Ambush Spot

The bounty hunters thought they had won the battle, and out of eager pursuit, they rushed, chasing the pirates to the fort. It was a heated chase by the bounty hunters, giving it all they had. They knew they had the victory! Then suddenly they were face to face with the unexpected, the blast of several cannons from the fort. The battle was over, the enemy was defeated because of their eagerness and greed for victory.

There had to be a cover-up of the enemy being in the swamp, ever, at all. It had to look like they died of fever, wild animals, starvation, or got lost. The bodies had to be disposed of in a way that would never show. If they were buried, someone could dig them up. If thrown in the swamp, their bones would show. Evidence would show how they were killed. What was the answer?

Joe Jo said he had the answer! He reminded the Captain of the large warm water pool that had the gators in it. Throw the bodies into the pool and the gators would eat the bodies plus most of the bones. That would take   care of most of the four hundred plus men that were killed. As for the enemy that was wounded and had survived, they will give them the choice to join them or be thrown to the gators. That would give those prisoners a chance to be free men by choice. And if they tried to leave? Then they would have to deal with the judgment of the swamp!

Gator Pool

Captain Strader thought that was a great idea and said they would start right away. Almost all the dead were already collected and set on the side of the bank of the swamp ... by the enemy. Some of the animals had drug some of the dead off, so they had to search for the remains.

When the dead were taken care of, Captain Drake began getting the people ready for the trip to their new home. It was summer now. This would make it hard to get ready for winter. All fifty-three of the wounded enemy decided to join the rest of the camp with joy; they were excited.

They had a lot of healing to do, not only with their bodies but also with their hearts and minds. They would learn to love these wonderful people because these people learn to give to each other; they had to.

CAPTAIN DRAKE STRADER

CHAPTER FOUR
Settling into the New Goshen Swamp Camp

The night before, the men had everything loaded and packed ready to go at early sunrise. When the sun rose in the east the next morning and it was light enough to see, they made their way to their new home and final resting place for most.

The trip was hard, as usual, but the water was not too high as it was fall and cooler. The boats worked well and carried their loads with no problem. The group was divided into three sections, so if they made a wrong turn, the whole group would not go down the wrong way. Some could stay back while the others had to turn back.

They didn't expect this trip to take just a few days. The Captain was expecting about six weeks or longer and was sending out scouts looking for good spots to camp. He had some men looking for fresh meat. They were well stocked with food and water, but they always took advantage of any extra food.

The good times couldn't last, and it began raining after the first week, lasting for three days. When it did stop, the weather was clear and warm and good for travel. They were making good time when they came upon a large beaver dam. Captain Drake Strader decided it would be easier and quicker to blow the dam with gun powder. The dam was blown and cleared, causing no problems, and they were on their way again.

Four weeks had passed, and they had gone through cold weather, rainy weather, and windy cold weather.

Things had warmed up to the fifties and clear today, everyone was in high spirits.

Joe Jo and the other scouts brought back good reports they had made good time. It looked like they could be home in around ten days. One of the problems they were facing was that the closer they got to their new home, the more they saw larger bears and the more sightings they had of the Sasquatch.

The Sasquatch were moving in more numbers now with movement being seen and heard at night. One thing the pirates figured out is their night vision is very good. They move at will during the night. They don't seem to want to have a confrontation with the men, yet they will fight if they are forced to. They do come into the camp at times, and wreck the place, just looking for food they smell. This is one group you do not want to make war with!

The Captain has given orders not to fire at them unless they show themselves aggressive to the point of harming someone. Then they have to protect themselves and their families at all cost.

Now the trip is going slowly as they are getting close to their new home. When they move a small tree across the way, it doesn't seem so small now. Now it seems that it takes longer to move it.

Finally, they have landed along the bank to set up camp for the last night. Tomorrow they will be at their new home and will be finally free. They are so deep into Goshen Swamp that only someone with knowledge of how to get in and out will be able to find them. There will only be the need for three or four watchmen to stay far down the swamp, looking for anyone stumbling by. That chance is very rare, yet they can't afford to take that chance when it would take only three or four men a week at a time to be safe.

The next morning at sunrise everyone got ready at daylight and set out. It was about noon when they arrived at the new location. They couldn't believe their eyes! It was better than they had been told. It was on high ground with a large spring feeding a small waterfall that fed a pond of fresh water filled with fish, and the water was drinkable. It was like a paradise, and as they came to the entrance, there was a large granite stone with a flat side facing the entrance.

The Water Fall

The Captain, after everyone had moved their things into the camp area, had their stone smith chisel on the stone:

CAMP OF THE
MAIDEN'S SKULL
OCTOBER 30, 1707
SUNDAY at 11:53 a.m.
ENTERED, THEN
SETTLED

Everyone was very pleased with Captain Drake Strader and what he had accomplished, bringing them so far with his dream. Something they thought could never have happened, this place was real!

They set up camp for the night and would rest later the next day. When the sun came up, it was a beautiful day, and almost everyone was busy at work. Things had to be unloaded, organized, and put away for storage until a proper place could be built. By the end of the day, things were in place as the Captain ordered. Now, they would get a good meal, and with plenty of rest, they would be ready for anything.

Daylight came early; the men started building homes like before, but this time they built them stronger to last longer. They had stones to build the chimneys this time, even though they had to travel a distance for some of the homes.

It was good having a lot of freshwater, with fresh fish nearby that didn't have a little taste of mud.

There were a lot of clearings close by that animals grazed in often especially deer, bear, and wild hogs along with a combination of other game and large birds. The swamp was full of life, everywhere things were going on. Gators, snakes, birds, beaver, and beautiful flowers were everywhere, and there was sunlight.

When fishing, if you found the right fishing hole, you could sit in the boat or on the bank and fish an hour with ease pulling fish out as fast as you could bait your hook. These were not little fish, but large, full-grown fish. People always came home with a long string of fish.

This was truly, what everyone was looking for, they could settle here and be happy. They were now ready to start building homes for the future. There were stones around for the fireplaces, the community ovens, and fire pits for barbecuing. Things this time would be built to last, not temporary. The ground was solid in most places to build on, with clearings to grow crops and a garden. They would need plenty of scarecrows because of the animals. Captain Strader decided to send some scouts to the trading post for supplies and to pick up some good dogs and guineas. The guineas would clear the land of ticks, leeches, and flees and cut down on flies and other pests. The dogs would help warn of wild beasts approaching and guard the fields. The guineas are great in so many ways and are impossible to catch by hand. You have to set a trap to catch them, and just any trap won't work. You have to be very cunning and deceptive.

The scouts made the trip, taking about eight weeks. The trip would be faster the next time, knowing the way better. They did get everything they went after and the dogs were fine-looking.

Guinea

It didn't take long, and the guineas went to work, pecking at the ground as if they could see food everywhere. They were as good as watchdogs also, sounding out their loud squawks with a rapid rhythm continuously at the appearance or sound of anything strange. This, along with the dogs, sent the predator away usually, but bears and other large beasts didn't scare as easily.

They did finally finish the houses in time for the winter, and everyone will work on them in their spare time. They did not have enough firewood cut for the winter, so men would be sent to cut firewood. They would have to have men go out to hunt and fish when possible. They still have plenty from their last settlement and should do well through the winter.

Everyone had their homes; now they wanted to build Captain Drake Strader the finest house that a pirate had ever lived in. Captain Strader said that he was very humbled by their desire, but for now, what he needed was a small house. Later, when all the work was completed, they could then take their time and build him the house of their desires.

Everyone agreed. Then Captain Drake said that he didn't think they needed to build a fort like before. They were so deep in the swamp that they could go back and fight at the old camp if necessary.

As for the wild animals and the beast that would come into the camp, they would be welcome as long as they didn't cause any really bad problems. The pirates may even begin to like having them around. As for the wild beast, that will be different, and they will build guard shacks up on stilts, above the ground, giving the guards good eyesight for a distance.

If they see or hear a wild beast near the camp, they will set fire to a brush pile, with timbers on it. The fires should keep the animals away for the rest of the night, because animals are frightened of the fire, especially at night. There will be several brush piles around the camp, and they will set only the ones they need to.

If this doesn't work, and it gets to be a real problem, then they will have to cut posts and set them into the ground around the camp. Hopefully this will not have to be done.

They can set the guard shacks all around the camp, in sight of each other.

Captain Strader is a man with a lot of foresight and wisdom, a good problem solver. He knows his men well. He knows each man's background, what he hates and what he loves. He would give his life for any of his men and they for him! He is the father and mother none of them ever had, and he is giving them something no one would dare try to give, their freedom!

This was it, their home, and they were determined to make the best life a person could have with it. Most of them had wives, some had children, and now the rest could think about children of their own for the first time in their lives.

Captain Drake called everyone together and said that they next needed to build a large barroom for their meetings and casual get-togethers and room for dancing. There were over 225 people in the camp now with the prisoners who had joined them. They, too, were as much a part of the group as the rest were now. They had to build shelters for the animals: the water buffalo, milk cows, and dogs. The guineas pretty much stayed in the trees, so if they needed a dry spot they never had a problem finding one. They were about the toughest bird one could find, and they multiply pretty rapidly.

The next day they slept late till about mid-morning and finally got started. Some of the scouts said they knew where they could get some good stones to make a large fireplace. This fireplace could be large enough to cook for a large group. They would also have the grill and the barbecue pit outside. One thing for sure, these people know how to eat and enjoy themselves.

Several months went by, and winter was harsh and hard on almost everyone, but everyone survived. It was well into the spring now, and another year was gone. It was now Saturday, June 23, 1708, and a spring shower had just fallen, settling the dust and freshening the air. It made everything feel so refreshed.

Captain Drake kept a log of everything that went on with the camp and the people in it. It was their history and their story to be told in the future. Anyone who wished could write his own copy of the logbook and take it home with him or when he left the camp. First they would take an oath, swearing never to let it be heard or seen or put it into the hands of an outsider. Only to be read to children or grandchildren and passed on only to them using the same oath. To them, this logbook was as sacred as the Holy Bible, and as time went on, they could come back and add to it.

You may think that these pirates could not read and write. Captain Drake Strader taught each of his men not only how to read and write but how to do so in several languages.

Spring brought a new spirit of life with it, everyone was so happy. During the past several months, there were problems with the beast coming close to the camp. Yet the brush fires did the job, and there were no problems. They never saw any reason to add the posts around the camp. The other animals came and went as they pleased, and some even became like pets. The kids found out by feeding the squirrels, rabbits, deer, and raccoons that they would come to them.

It was truly a paradise in the fullest sense. No one would ever have thought that inside Goshen Swamp was such a place as this.

The people decided it was time to build Captain Drake Strader a home he could be proud of. They got together, making the plans: it had to be near the waterfall, two-story at least with the finest stones they could find, the best cedars, white oak, black oak, hickory, black maple, walnut, cherry, and every kind of wood that can be found or bought. And dried for as long as needed, they were in no hurry. It was going to be built right. The furniture was going to be made from the finest wood available, not from just one kind but several kinds and the quality that was found in the most expensive homes. Captain Drake could dine with Royalty at his home if he wished when it was finished.

It was nine months and three weeks later, Wednesday, December 10, 1710, when they completed Captain Strader's home and he moved in. It was a marvel of a home, nothing to be compared to in the Carolinas, and it was hidden.

The Captain was so impressed by the joy of his people that

he broke down in tears and wept like a baby, uncontrolled. This was the first time he had ever shown any emotion of any kind to his people, especially his men. They loved him so much more!

It was now the middle of January, and the Captain decided it was time to go to Beautancus to get some supplies and do some more trading. Trading was always good at the trading post at Beautancus. Even the local farmers had a good selection, plenty of good vegetables and fruits if available.

They always left with their wagons loaded, wagons they had traded for years earlier. Their water buffalo pulled the wagons and then pulled the boats. They would hide the wagons in the brush at the edge of the swamp. So far no one had bothered them. This time, while at the trading post, they got a real big surprise. They just couldn't wait to get to camp to tell Captain Strader. They took a copy of a poster that stated,

All pirates in North Carolina wanting amnesty should report to the Governor's office in Raleigh, N.C., before the end of the year 1711. They would have to pledge their allegiance to the British Crown, obey all laws of the British Crown and the Colony of North Carolina, and give up all weapons and ships.

Now Captain Drake had to go to Raleigh to see if it was really true or not. If so, he would ask for some of the other men to come and register also. If everything went well, he would send for others to come later, until all had registered. Then they could choose to stay at the camp or leave; that would be their decision only. First, they had to make sure it was true and not a trap!

A couple of days later, Captain Drake Strader with six men and a couple of water buffalo, headed out for Raleigh, N.C., to see the Governor. Hoping to get amnesty for his 225 + men and women that had joined him. He did have a few things he wanted to ask for in exchange. By chance, he might get his request.

They traveled back to the entrance to Goshen Swamp, hooked the buffalo to the two wagons, and headed to Raleigh.

They arrived in Raleigh at dusk, setting up camp on the outside of town. It was a grove of oak trees growing together, and it would help keep the wind down and the snow off of them.

The next morning they had an early breakfast, moving around trying to keep warm by the fire. Captain Strader decided to take one of his most loyal men with him and go to the Governor's office. They went to town and bought new clothes, shoes, and hats, trying to look presentable.

When he arrived, he was warmly welcomed and asked to sit. He was told that the Governor would be a while, but he would see him. The Governor was a while, almost two hours, but he finally did see the Captain.

Captain Drake told the Governor who he was, why he was there, and the number of people he was representing.

The Governor was quite impressed, he was aware of who Captain Drake Strader was and of his record.

The Captain also pointed out that in the last five years or better, neither he nor any of his men had been active in the piracy business. They have been living deep in the swamps of North Carolina, living happy successful lives and bothering no one for over five years. What they were asking for was lifelong amnesty and the right to 2,800 acres of swampland in Goshen Swamp at the Captain's designation. He asked that it be tax-free for life for the families because it is worthless land, a wasteland, good for nothing to no one but them.

The Governor stared hard at the Captain for a minute, thinking. Then he said, "Let me go into my study and do some research and more thinking. I'll be back."

After a little over an hour, he came back. After doing his research, he said he would pass the idea to his trustees. If they liked the idea, it was settled and he would make him an appointment for tomorrow afternoon. As far as he was concerned, it was a good idea.

The next afternoon Captain Drake met with the Governor, and he said that he met with his advisers. They did not accept the idea at first, but when he explained that they had been inactive in piracy for over five years, they decided to do it.

The Governor said it would take a week to draw up the proper documents. So he made another appointment for the following week.

Captain Drake and the men spent some time traveling around the city, looking at the different buildings and statues.

"This city had to have a lot of money going through it at one time," said one of the men.

Captain Drake said, "Yes, and it still does!" The week was well spent around the city, getting its history and layout.

Now it was time for their appointment. Captain Drake Strader and his companions were ready to sign their amnesty papers. They each would sign the documents for the 2,800 acres of land deeded to them in Goshen Swamp. The Captain was given his copies of the papers and each man received a copy of his amnesty papers. They joyfully left, looking forward to their trip home to tell the others the good news.

When they finally got back home, it was February and snowing with a little freezing rain. This time it was really home, and the others couldn't believe how beautiful the amnesty papers were and that it was real. They were totally surprised to find out that they, as a body, owned 2,800 acres of land for the first time in their life.

They would never be able to borrow money on the land because it was worthless, yet to them it was priceless. No one would ever know how precious this land would be to these people and their young. They would never have to ask permission to do anything to the land or their homes or travel the seas with its storms and winds to fear. Captain Drake set up a large party to go to Raleigh the next morning. One of the men that went with him   will go with the group and show them around town and where to file for their papers. As soon as they return another group would go to Raleigh and return until everyone was registered.

By August 12, 1711, all persons at the camp were registered and had a copy of their amnesty papers. They had all beat the deadline! Now some would decide if they wanted to stay in the swamp or give up everything and leave, taking a chance of not being able to return. There were twenty-two men, all single, including some of the prisoners, that decided to leave.

The next day, there was a meeting in the barroom with everyone, and they all said their goodbyes. The men told them where they thought they would go to spend the rest of their lives. Some said they might go back to being merchant seaman if it didn't work out otherwise. They all said they would stay out of prison. Caption Drake had given them a good education, which would go far for them.

They left just after mid-morning, heading to a new destination and a new way of life. Hopefully, this new beginning would prove fruitful for all involved.

Joe Jo came in from a hunting trip that day and said he saw an extremely large footprint, similar to that of a man, in the swamp. He followed it off and on for close to three days before finding the final stopping place. It was a large hairy creature with a big head, about nine to ten feet tall, and had a big hairy chest. The Captain said that it sounds like Sasquatch and what the other men have described, but no one has gotten that close before.

The Captain was eager to see where this camp was. Joe Jo said there were about three or four families with several young. He saw about three or four males and what looked like three females. He made drawings of them quickly, then he got out of there as soon as he could, making his way back to the camp and giving his report.

The next day they made their way out early, at about daylight. Going down the swamp waters in the boats, they would be gone for days, maybe a couple of weeks. The Captain was taking Joe Jo and five other men with him. This trip could be mighty dangerous, going into uncharted territory that only Joe Jo had been in once. He did mark his way with the ax, cutting a slice of bark out of a tree now and then. Finally, they came to the point that they had to leave the boats on the bank. Then they followed the bank, crossing flat land now and then, and then backcrossing the swamp again. This goes on and on till dark, and they decide to climb up into the trees and get some sleep till morning.

When morning came they started out again, following the tree line at the edge of the swamp. They can make faster time now. The trees being marked saved a lot of time, and they are watching the Sasquatch as they go about doing their daily duties. It is amazing how compassionate they are and able to comfort one another.

The Captain realized it was getting late and time to go; it would be getting dark before they knew it. They slowly slipped out and were on their way, thinking they were in the clear. Then suddenly a big male Sasquatch crashed through the brush grabbing two men at one time, throwing one against a tree and the other tearing his chest open with his hands. Captain Drake fired a shot and hit him in his chest, but it did not slow him down. He then grabbed another man, breaking his neck with one quick jerk of his body.

Then he tore his body apart like it was a doll. Joe Jo fired a shot hitting him in the side, then he took his hatchet and struck him in the head as he fell to his side. The blow never phased him. He grabbed Joe Jo, throwing him to the ground, breaking his arm and a rib. Captain Drake was on the Sasquatch backstabbing him with his knife, then being thrown back. The other men had been thrown to the bushes, trees, and rocks and they, too, were injured. Sasquatch finally got to his feet and ran off. He attacked because they were so close to his camp.

The men got together and left as quickly as they could; not being able to carry the dead, they decided to come back the next day for them. The next day Captain Drake took ten men, well equipped for the trip, and went back to collect the dead.

The trip was long again, even longer this time because Joe Jo could not go with them; he had injuries. They finally came to the spot where the dead men were. These men had seen death before but nothing like this. It put a fear in them like they never knew. They thought the stories the other men told were exaggerated and couldn't be true, but now they thought differently. When they saw the area, how it was destroyed and the trees had their limbs broken, with brush uprooted, then seeing the bodies, they were in a hurry to leave. They couldn't believe how anyone survived that attack.

Finding someone to help carry out the dead bodies is usually a problem. These men were in such a hurry to get out of there, the men had the bodies bagged and ready to go before the Captain was.

When they did reach the camp, they wasted no time preparing the bodies for cremation. Both bodies were placed on brush and a large log fire for each man. The Captain gave a thirty-minute history about the men doing their service with him and how brave they were to their death. Everyone yelled "FAREWELL BROTHERS." Then the fires were set as the sun was going down in the Goshen Swamp.

The reason they were cremated is that the water level in the swamp is so high they have no soil deep enough to bury someone.

These were the first men killed since the eleven that died when they attacked the Dutch ship. That is a very good record for a Captain in the high seas who then had the battles in the swamps. The Captain had a very good doctor, and the Captain made sure that he was kept up to date with all the latest medical journals he desired.

One of the men who died was married, and the other was single. They were both hard-working men that were respected. The widow had no children. She remained unmarried for some time, then she married and had a daughter and other children. Everyone was very supportive of the family.

The camp is growing with children and the other children that first came are grown and have their own children. They have kids of all grade levels with good educations.

The men, when they go hunting and fishing, make sure that Sasquatch is nowhere around. If he is anywhere to be found, they find a good hiding spot till they know that he is gone. Then they will carefully make their way out to look for game. He always has first place at the hunting fields.

Old Man Morgan and his wife, Lisa, left the camp years ago taking with them his recipe for the mosquito repellant. Captain Drake told him he would need the document for his copyright if he was going to market it. He did get a lifetime copyright and a patent in the USA, England, Spain, and France. Delmar Morgan and Lisa Morgan became extremely rich people, taking their wealth and paying for college for any child wanting to go to college in Raleigh or elsewhere.

The Morgans were a common sight, going into the swamp about every six weeks. They always took gifts for the children, with special gifts for their devoted friends. They always stayed with Captain Drake Strader, the camp had given him his own daytime and nighttime servants. This was out of their appreciation for what he did for them. The servants' jobs were rotated only as they wished.

It is now Tuesday, April 5, 1735, and the people are settled down, living a quiet and happy life. Things are slow and at a steady pace with no mosquitoes, thanks to Old Man Morgan's repellant spread around the camp. The camp has grown a lot, and after the run-in with the male Sasquatch, Captain Drake decided to build a wall around the camp. Not with posts but with stone, large stone, no matter how far they have to go to get them, it is that important. The gate will have to be made of double-strength, large cypress trees that will be strong and last. It will open from the inside, then push open to the outside, back to back.

It will take several men to open and close the gates. The gates will be open during the day and closed at night.

Any animals that want to come in must come in during the day. The stone wall will be set as deep as they can set it in the wet ground for a foundation.

The wall was finished, and they did have wild bears come up to the wall and the gate, but they gave up. There was no contest. They were like baby cubs scratching at the gate trying to get in.

They were confident they could hold off Sasquatch, firing their weapons at him while he tried to tear down the gate. He could stand only so much and he would have to leave or die. He was clever and had good instincts. Captain Drake said if they had a problem with Sasquatch, it would be only once if they kept him out. After thinking about it, the Captain said that they usually had hot water boiling in the two pots for washing clothes or sterilizing. So instead of shooting the Sasquatch, they would pour boiling water on him; this would be one thing he would remember and not forget. It would leave a bad taste in his mouth for a long time to come.

About five or six weeks later, it was just a little after dark as everyone was finishing eating. Sasquatch came sniffing around the stone wall, checking its strength and finely getting to the gate. By this time the guards had informed the Captain of what was going on. So the Captain had the boiling water ready when Sasquatch started banging on the gate. The men soaked him down with the hot water, and he ran off into the swamp screaming. That proved to be very effective, and there were no more problems with Sasquatch. They did have problems with different bears, over and over.

The gate did prove to hold its strength with no problem or showing any weakness. The way it was built, it would last in working order for over eighty years, maybe over a hundred or more. Time would tell. These people had plans to stay here for a long time. They were a growing nation of people of many nationalities with many children for a long future.

Many years went by, and most of the old pirates had died and were cremated like the ones killed by Sasquatch.

For each person that died, young or old, a stone marker was set up for them in their memory.

It had their name, date of birth if known, date of death, and a word or two from Captain Drake. Their graveyard was growing to some size by this time.

Captain Drake himself was sick. He had been laid up in his bed for about two weeks. He was just tired and old; he had run his course in life. He had lived an exciting life, and now it was time to turn the responsibilities over to someone else. Everyone knew who that would be, his loyal companion and the one he had trained as a young man. The one who had learned to walk, act, and think like Captain Drake Strader.

He was the young Italian born on the Maiden's Skull in 1700. Now he was 61 years old and ready to lead the camp of the 328 survivors of the Maiden's Skull. He, too, had children of his own, four boys and two girls. Captain Drake Strader appointed him as Captain Rocca Lombardi, but most called him Captain Rock because that is what his name means in Italian.

Captain Strader lived two days longer and died in his sleep. Outside his home was a garnet stone inscribed with his name, date of birth, September 1, 1676, and date of death April 10, 1761, then a list of dedications from his men.

His body was placed in a garnet stone coffin which was sealed and placed in his study. There were also his swords, his two pistols, and his several guns and knives left out on display about the room. He was buried with his favorite uniform dress and attire.

His treasure chest and all his wealth were considered his and left in his home. Anyone breaking into the home to steal his valuables would be thrown to the gators alive, no questions asked!

The home was locked and sealed; the doors and all windows were never to be entered again by anyone, for any reason, and that was understood by everyone, young and old. His home would be kept in good condition at all times. Always on a scheduled basis, his home would be repaired and kept cleaned as long as the camp existed.

CAPTAIN ROCCA LOMBARDI

CHAPTER FIVE
The First Generations Raised in Goshen Swamp, North Carolina

On Friday, April 10, 1761, Captain Drake Strader died in his sleep during the early morning. Before his death, he had appointed his long-time friend, Rocca Lombardi, who was born on the Maiden's Skull, Captain Drake Strader's pirate ship, to be the new Captain of the camp at Goshen Swamp, with full authority over everything. Everyone was to give him the same respect that they did Captain Strader.

Captain Rocca began his duties on Friday morning, conducting the funeral arrangements for Captain Strader, then beginning the arrangements for the Captain's home. He was to call a meeting of everyone to the barroom, where he would try to explain that there would be no changes in the way things would be run. It would run the same as if Captain Drake were still there.

This is just what the people expected; Captain Rocca had always been by the Captain's side and knew how he wanted everything done, anyway. The men wanted to know if it would be ok to call him Captain Rock, since everyone knew him as Rock, anyway. He said, no problem!

Captain Rock grew up with three other friends that were extremely loyal to each other and especially to Rock. There was Orsin, the oldest, whom they called Bear. Then there was Luka

Barlow; he was active and full of energy and always moving around. Finally, there was Bruno, the youngest of the four. He, too, was Italian and was the stoutest and the strongest, by far.

Captain Rock had married Sarah, and they had six children, several grandchildren, and a few greatgrandchildren. Orsin married Tessa, and they, too, had a large family as did most of the others. Luka and Bruno had married younger wives because there were no girls their ages when growing up. Times were too hard to think about having children back then.

Today, they were multiplying like flies. It was the good times, and they had made it, yet the young ones were getting restless. They didn't know what it was like on the outside and how well they were protected.

Many young ones, when they became of age, got the itch and had to see the world for themselves. They wanted to get involved and see the things they had read and studied about. Turns out many did leave on their adventures to discover the world. Some that left came back, regretting that they ever left. Yet, at the same time, they said it was good they got it out of their system and got to see what it was like. It was different from what they were expecting, more people and traffic were moving around town. Some said it might be nice to go to Raleigh in eight to ten years for a change but not to live.

The first thing that Captain Rock said they needed to do was to remodel the homes. They had all weathered and run down over the years, both inside and outside. The roofs needed repair also. The chimneys had held up and were in really good shape for the years.

All the other buildings would need repair; the medical shed, guard shacks, smokehouses, and then later, the home of Captain Strader, which was in good shape as usual anyway. Every six months the people did a thorough cleaning and repair of his home, top to bottom.

It took a little over a year, but they finally finished cleaning everything up and doing the repairs. In all these years the camp had never had any problem with intruders again. Just a few stories of pirates that tried to live in the swamp and got swept away with the mysteries of Goshen Swamp, never to be seen or heard of again.

These men would go hunting and, taking the dogs, they could track bear, wild cats, deer, almost anything they wanted except Sasquatch. Sasquatch had been off-limits for many years. These dogs were trained when to bark and when not to, when to play dead and when to fight. They were trained to do anything their master wanted or needed at the time. They were offspring of the ones they purchased from the trading post years before.

It was early in the morning on an October day with a steady drizzle of rain and a chill in the air just right for hunting deer. The dogs were very uneasy and excited. Then suddenly a big bear sprang from behind them, running. She attacked the dogs first and then the three men before they could get off a shot. The dogs attacked the bear, keeping it busy while the men got their guns and wounded the bear.

The bear staggered off weakly. The men were hurt a little, but one dog was dead and another was hurt but could go on. They were really angry and upset; this bear was not going to get away. They set out tracking the bear and found it lying next to a cub, dead.

They knew that if they left the cub, it would starve or be killed by other beasts. So they decided to bring it back to the camp with them and raise it till it was old enough to live on its own. The men took the dead mother, hung her in a tree, skinned her, cut the meat into sections, and headed home.

Arriving at the camp, they were greeted by several men that were expecting them much sooner. Surprised that they were injured, they quickly took them to the medical shed. Captain Rock wanted to know what had happened and why they brought back the bear cub. They then explained why and that the meat was in the boat with the skin.

The bear cub was a male, and the kids went crazy over it.

They had to build it a house and a pen to stay in, so it would not wander off. Problem was, the kids kept letting it out to play with it. They did not let it wander off, and they did put it back in its pen when they finished playing. They gave him the name Benny first thing.

Going out in the swamp was always an adventure. While scouting out an area, looking for wild boars, Luka fell into quicksand and was sinking quickly when Bruno threw him a rope and pulled him out just before his head went under.

Wild Boar

That is just how close they could come to losing their life, in a few seconds. Quicksand can appear as plain sand on the surface of the ground and can take a man before he knows what has happened, or it can take him slowly. Animals are saved just on their strength, endurance, and ability to move out of that situation.

Luka was pulled to solid ground and got his footing, but he was very weak. They continued on their hunt, finally coming across a group of wild hogs. They selected the healthiest in the group with the most meat and shot it, making sure to bleed it properly.

They cut a strong pole, tied the hog on it, and carried it back to the boat. Then they headed back to the camp. When they got back, others had returned with several deer and another bear. There was a lot of food in the swamp, so they never went hungry.

Another year and a half had gone by. The bear cub was no longer a cub. It had been let loose for some time, but it never left. It continued to hang around the camp, never traveling very far away. The food was just too good here, and he didn't have to work for it. The kids still played with him, and the men figured out how to get him to carry firewood tied to his back and in his arms. They changed his name from Benny to Ben when he grew up. They did build him a bigger shed with stone and timbers, making him feel more at home outside the camp.

When mating season came around, he would wander off for a spell but always came home. Some of the men saw Ben during mating season catching fish to eat when they were out on their hunting trip.

The men did not go near Ben as he was in the wild, and there were other bears around. They decided to back away and go home the way they came. When they got back, they told the others they saw Ben and he was healthy and looking good. That made them all feel so excited to hear about Ben. Ben has become as big a part of the family like any of the children. It would be a great loss if something were to happen to him.

Finally, mating season is over and Ben has come back home to the kids and his chores. The kids are all excited and ready to give their time and attention to Ben. The whole camp is glad to see Ben back because while he was gone, something felt misplaced.

Ben was about five years old now. He did whatever he wanted to do but was still a big baby. He moved about in the swamp with ease, having nothing to fear and catching catfish as if they were lying out to catch. Finding berries for the women to pick was a gift. All they had to do was lead him into the swamp where there should be some, they then give him some to eat, and he went straight to the bushes for them. While they picked, he would eat.

While the women were picking berries, a mother bear with

her cubs came near and attempted to attack the women. Ben suddenly came to their defense and stopped the mother bear by attacking her. He had a violent battle with the mother bear, finally driving her away with her cubs. Ben was hurt but not seriously, and the women were not hurt at all, just scared to death.

Taking the many berries that they had collected they made their way back to camp. Ben led the way, and they never had to worry about getting lost. They got back early and had time to rest before they got ready for supper. Many things were going on in the camp. They had just gotten a new printing press for the camp newspaper   and the school. The people were excited about that; now they could read the papers and the ink was not smeared, nor were the words running together.

They had a small church that had been built for many years. It was not a denomination but just a church for anyone. No cross, no star, no nothing just a large Bible that belonged to Captain Drake Strader, and he always had it opened and underlined at Psalms 83:18:

That men may know that thou, whose name alone is Jehovah, art the most high over all the earth. (KJV)

This camp had grown into a community with a general store for small items like axes, handles, salt, sugar, coffee, tobacco, and other necessaries. The smokehouse was an addition to it, too. They were responsible for organizing the trips to the trading post and keeping the store stocked with supplies.

Hunting parties were always going out and never to the same spot. They didn't want to kill all the local game in an area but give them time to build up and to restock the herds and the flocks. That was only good hunting sense for the future, and after all, they had 2,800 acres to hunt.

They went by to check the alligator pool to see what it had done over the years. It had done quite well and spread out to the swamp, there were many other gators around the area now. They killed one to take back to camp to see how the meat would taste.

They decided it would be ok if they were to run low on food but not for daily use.

They had to travel a little farther out to get firewood now and had to cut down the larger cypress trees closer to camp. That meant they would lose shade in the summer and a lot of the cool breeze. The women started complaining to Captain Rock about the men cutting trees for firewood, and he had it stopped. They only had a couple cut down when he had it stopped.

A few weeks later everyone was having a dance in the barroom, celebrating the fiftieth anniversary of their marriage, when a lantern was knocked over on some burlap sacks and a fire was started. It was next to the door and only about three-fourths of the people got out unharmed. Some had taken in so much smoke they could hardly breathe. Others had been burned badly along with breathing problems. They didn't think some would live. They managed to get everyone out, but many were in bad shape. They were placed along the side of the pool and being treated the best they knew how. The medical shed was filled with the worst cases and treated by the doctor and his staff as best as they knew how with what they had. This was the first time anything like this had ever happened to the camp. They were caught completely unprepared!

If they had only had a back door, there would have been no casualties. Next time there would be a back door wide enough for everyone to get out in case of another fire in the building.

Some did die because of the fire. As to the cause, no one knew exactly what happened except that the lantern was knocked over. That was what started the fire, which caused the destruction and death. No one set the fire, it was just one of those things that happen.

The only thing left of the building was what was built of stone and granite. Captain Rock said that they would start rebuilding the barroom just as soon as everyone felt it was a good time. This time, it would be better than it was before since now they knew what they needed extra and where it was needed.

It wasn't long before the barroom was complete and in use

again. Everyone was back to having a good time partying, singing, playing games, and getting back to normal. Some still had that long stare into the darkness, that quietness in their deep soul you could not reach that fear of the fire they still had, as if they were lost and couldn't be reached!

They were the ones the camp would have to be especially careful with, to help and care for. Everyone was hurt, but for some, it cut deeper than others. Will they ever understand? Some things you can understand, then others are so deep in their mind that they can't be reached. You can only try to be there, just "be there," saying nothing, That is all … to that person, that quiet time is priceless with someone who really cares. Someone there who feels what you feel and wants to cry with you and can't, saying nothing.

This is caused by trauma that affects a person's deeper heart, mind, and soul. So deep, people don't know how to reach the problem to help. It is nothing new and is found mostly with men of wars.

Time goes on, and Captain Rock's children mostly leave the camp and go outside to Raleigh or Charlotte to live. Several others in the camp decide to leave and look for a new life outside Goshen Swamp. The camp is getting smaller but there are still a large group of people.

The trading post at Beautancus had now grown to two trading posts, and both were very prosperous, giving the men more to bargain for and choose from. Growth was starting to spring up everywhere on the outside. People were coming and going from all over the country; the Carolinas were growing fast. It was getting harder to hide the idea that the pirates' next generations existed.

People at the trading post were impressed with the people from the swamp. They were always clean, well educated, clever, and had good furs and pelts, never trying to cheat anyone or cause any trouble. Yet, they did prove one evening that they would not back down from a fight. Three of the men beat five men who were much bigger than they half to death. Since then, they have never been bothered. Two of the men were sons of Bruno, and like their father, they were very strong.

They usually came in with some of their women who were spoken of as very good-looking. That was how the fight started. The five men decided they were going to party with their women. Never again did anyone dare to approach the women that came with these men. People never forgot what those men looked like when the three men were finished.

The trading post where the fight happened had a drawing of the fight framed on its wall. This was to remind any strangers coming into the trading post to be aware. The people that were coming in from the camp were known as Swampers and had respect from the people in the area, as well as the local farmers. They were known to trade with them from time to time for fresh food they couldn't get at the trading post.

Luka had a son born in his later years; his wife was much younger than he was, so he could have a son in his older years. People were afraid that at his age the child may not be normal. The opposite happened, and his child was a normal boy who grew up to be a genius. His name was Jarrett Barlow. Jarrett was at the top of his class in school, taking all the different languages and challenging math he could. When he graduated, he went on to a large college up north, getting a better education.

When he left for college, his father went to his father's treasure chest and gave him enough gold to pay for his schooling and an expense account. Jarrett was gone for twelve years, finishing college with honors. He had taken medical, some surgery, basic chemistry, and forestry.

Jarrett was offered many well-paying jobs in the industrial world, which would have made him a rich man. He could have opened a medical office up north and become a wealthy man. Jarrett, being the humble man that he was, decided to go back to his roots at Goshen Swamp in North Carolina.

Jarrett set up his practice with their doctor at the camp in Goshen Swamp, giving up a life of leisure and wealth. He was happier with his family and the lifelong friends he could trust.

Ben had gotten up in years, and one day he left and never came back. The Captain said he must have just gone off somewhere and died. He had gotten to where he weighed around five hundred pounds. He was so large, the kids could not play games with him very much anymore.

Orsin and Bruno had died some years ago, making all the ones on the Maiden's Skulls gone except for Captain Rock, and he was lying on his death bed at ninety-two. The date was January 12, 1792, when he died. He did appoint Jarrett Barlow as the camp Captain before he died. No one in the camp objected, but all were very happy at the appointment.

Captain Barlow, set out to have every home and building sterilized with boiling water and soap along with all utensils and tools used, especially those used to serve food. The barroom was to be sterilized completely also.

Captain Strader's home was detailed every six months as regulated from the beginning anyway. It would never need sterilizing. No one was ever allowed in his house except every six months.

Captain Barlow put to work what he had learned about forestry in college. He had learned how to irrigate to grow crops in wet areas, like rice. They started growing rice, and they loved it. It was a good trading product that no one else had.

Something new would spring up on the outside world nearby that was not so common before. It was slavery.

More farmers were buying slaves. Farther south it was more common, and some farms had as many as a hundred slaves.

Captain Barlow meet with his advisers, and they decided that there would never be any slaves in the camp of the free pirates. That decree was put into the document that Captain Drake Strader started and was kept by every Captain after him as a history of the camp.

Slavery was spreading fast in the south and had been for the past fifty years. Plantations were expanding to over a thousand acres with slaves working the crops. There were slave platforms set up for certain days of the week at Fayetteville, Raleigh, and

Charlotte, North Carolina.

Families were being broken up and sent to different farms, never to be seen or heard from again. These people had no rights at all and were not even considered human beings. They were considered lower than the Indians that most people hated.

Slaves had been in North Carolina since before the 1700s when the British encouraged slavery to grow more crops. Yet, in the last fifty years, it was getting very popular with the people. Some of the farmers were very cruel to their slaves, treating them as property, completely. Others treated their slaves as the Bible said to treat slaves and were kind to the ones deserving, carrying their load.

Several of the men and women were coming back from the trading post one day. They were approached by three black Negroes, begging for help. They were runaway slaves from a plantation further south. How could these people who were children of freedom themselves say no? Turns out there were twenty-eight of them, thirsty, hungry, and in rags. Taking them in, they went straight to Goshen Swamp.

They were not about to take them to the camp, most of them were sick and needing help. They decided to go to the fort and let them stay there. Finally, they reached the old fort and told everyone to stay there, it would be their home as long as they would like.

They were given instructions about keeping the gate closed at night, not leaving food out, and the many necessary things they needed to know. They could choose any house to live in that they wanted, and there were many to choose from.

A couple of scouts stayed behind and went out to kill a deer or two for them to eat and showed them where the springs were for their freshwater. Several boats were left behind at the fort that they could use. The men left them with food for a little while, till they could get back and kill more game for them.

The old man that was in charge of the slaves was named Jubal. His people had a lot of respect for him; he was very wise.

When the group reached the camp and told Captain Barlow

what had happened, he and Lester, the other doctor, packed their bags, and with some others, headed for the fort. When they arrived it was mid-morning a couple of weeks later, and they checked on those who were the sickest first. Several older men and women were just exhausted and sick with colds.

The doctors would need to stay at least a week before returning to the camp. Everyone had questions: Who were they? Where did they come from? How many were they? The questions did not stop and just kept on coming with no end.

The Captain sat down and had a long talk with Jubal and his advisers, explaining how serious it was that they obey all the rules. They had to build several brush piles with poles and logs for a fire if needed for monsters coming near or into the camp, day or night. They chuckled under their breath when he mentioned Sasquatch. The Captain said, "That's ok. You will see it if you make it a habit to leave leftover food outside."

The Captain and the men stayed nine days, showing the men slaves the hunting grounds and the best fishing holes and leaving them with four rifles, powder, and rifle balls to hunt with. There were a few old traps still left at the fort that could be used as well. When the Captain left he took a list with him for the general store of things the women would be needing.

When they reached the camp, there was a discussion about letting the slaves come on into the camp. After all, they had their freedom and land, and no one could take it from them. Why couldn't they tell the story of Captain Drake Strader and the lost camp in Goshen Swamp? Outsiders should be welcome to come in!

The Captain, in a rage, jumped up and asked, "What are you talking about? Do you have any idea what the 'greedy people' of this world would do to this camp if they knew where it was? They would kill the majority of us, looking for the treasures of Captain Drake Strader and his men. Your uncles and great uncles left their treasure chests, so you could go to college and for any necessary goods, like medical operations.

"These treasures are an abundance of wealth, getting more

valuable as time goes on. There will never again be any mention of the treasures again, especially the treasures of Captain Strader and what stays in his house. Anyone telling will be thrown alive into the alligators' pool!

"As for the slaves, they are sick, and we don't need their sicknesses. We will give them time to see for sure what their decision will be. The swamp is a hard place to live; we will see how badly they want their freedom. They will live for better than a year at the fort, then we will see what their thinking is like. Then I and my advisers will decide what is just for everyone."

It is summer and hot, and the kids want to swim in the freshwater pool at the bottom of the spring. It is a large pool but the Captain says no, absolutely not, it is for drinking water only. Swimming in it will make people sick, so they have to stay out. The people don't see the problem, because it is so HOT, and they don't want to understand. So the doctor explains that if the children pee in the pool, they will get sick. Then he asked, "Are you willing to drink someone else's pee?" The people became more understanding then.

The summer made it hard to get their game back to the camp with the heat and humidity. The men were so exhausted, it made it extra hard dragging the game to the boat. Sometime they had to fight off other beasts that would attack them and go after their kill when dragging it to the boat. One man had a bear attack him, stealing a large deer, breaking a couple of ribs, and giving him some deep scars. He managed to get away with his life, getting back to the boat and going to the camp for help.

One of the men learned not to let his string of fish float along behind his boat while going home. When he got home he found a good size turtle clinging to the last remaining fish he had. The turtle had eaten every fish on his line except the last one. He did grab the turtle before it got away and made a turtle stew, mixed with what was left of the fish.

The young men would take the young women out to the meadows, close to sundown, trying to charm them and impress them into becoming their ladies. There would usually be a deer, a covey of quail, rabbit, or a pair of doves to rob the moment of love, leaving the young man at a loss for words like he had to start all over, the mood is gone, it's different. Now, where does he start!

The young boys are busy in school and are continuing to learn like the ones who grew up ahead of them. No matter where they go or who they are around, they hear a foreign language that they know. Always when they are at the trading post, there are people needing help with their languages.

CAPTAIN JARRETT

CHAPTER SIX
More Generations Raised in Goshen Swamp, North Carolina

The slaves had been at the fort for a year and a half and had done very well for themselves. Jubal had kept his people well organized and happy. They felt safe for the first time in years and could sleep restfully; it felt good to them. These people were healthy, strong, and full of energy something they never had before in their lives.

74

They were enjoying themselves too much, getting too relaxed. Everyone had forgotten what Captain Jarrett told them about leftover food being left outside. They were not latching the gate with the trimmed logs, only with a strong board.

Early one morning, Sasquatch came looking for the leftovers he had been smelling. It had finally gotten the best of him, and he tore open the gate with little struggle. Coming inside the fort, he was tearing down porches and sheds, destroying anything in his way. The guards fired shots, but couldn't tell if they hit him or not. It didn't matter because it would take a couple of well-placed shots to bring him down, anyway.

He finally got to the grill and oven. After getting the food he wanted, he destroyed them both. Then Jubal came out of his house, grabbed a torch from the porch post, and threw it on the brush pile, setting it ablaze.

He then yelled for others to do the same. Finally the fires were burning and Sasquatch was trying to find a way out.

He threw a couple of men like they were rag dolls to the side. They thought they could jump on him and subdue him which was a bad mistake.

They got off with only bruises; Sasquatch was interested only in getting out, not a fight. He was scared of the fires. If it were not for the fires, there would have been a lot of people killed and seriously wounded.

They had met Sasquatch, and they were not laughing under their breath. This time Jubal realized the importance of following Captain Jarrett's instructions to the letter. The Captain had already experienced the dangers of the swamp and was passing on his advice. From then on things would be run a little stricter for the best of everyone.

After that, the guards paid a little more attention to the swamp noises. They reported the sounds of bears around the camp at night and said it might be good to keep guards on the lookout during the day for bears. It did happen that a couple of bears came wondering around the wall, sniffing and just being curious. Then one made his way to the gate, and it was open, so a couple of theguards fired and killed the bear. The other ran off into the swamp in fear and never looked back.

Everyone celebrated with a great meal of bear meat. They skinned the bear, making a bear coat for Jubal for the coming winter. This would keep him warm, and it also had pockets. He was so excited about the coat they made because he knew it was special.

Things were made more secure, and the people were again feeling happy and at ease. When going out hunting, the men remembered what Captain Jarrett said about seeing Sasquatch, "Just leave him alone. He will not bother you. Stay hidden." Now that they knew what to look for, they were seeing the Sasquatch more often when hunting.

The slaves were thinking more and more about the slaves they had left behind and about how nice it would be if they could join up with them at the fort. They spoke to Jubal about the idea, but he quickly said no and that the Captain said it would be out to leave. It would jeopardize the lives of over five hundred people with children. They could only think of themselves. This was their future now, and they had to make the best of it. They started with twenty-eight people and now there were thirty-two, all happy, healthy, and growing. The people had to stop being so hard-headed and stubborn and pay more attention to Jubal. The people did like Jubal and respected him, yet he was so easy going some took advantage of his good nature. His wife was constantly cautioning him about that and warning him of a certain man in the group named Ruman. Ruman was not a smart man but thought he was. He was more greedy than anything else and always wanted to be first among the group. Winter was on the way, and they were short of firewood. They needed to restock the brush piles in the fort also and get extra freshwater. Jubal said he was afraid it would be a cold winter in the damp swamp this year.

They did have good houses to live in; even if they were old, they were well built.

The swamp people had taught them well how to live off the swamp by hunting, fishing, and serving and by curing meat the proper way to keep it for long spells. They had learned how to grow crops in the swamp, fish with nets, and use traps. They could never have survived without their help.

There was still trouble in the group, although nothing really serious, concerning Jubal. It was Ruman he was always looking for a way out of the swamp, looking for something better. It had to do with "the grass being greener on the other side." That man was a dreamer.

Every time he decided he had found the way out, he got lost for a couple of days, coming back home scared to death that snakes, wild cats, badgers, and bears would get him before he could find his way home or find his way out. Each time he swore he would never do it again. Jubal thought that the last time scared him enough not to try it again for a long time. The wild cat and bear can scare a man pretty good deep in the swamp when he is lost. Captain Jarrett met with his advisors and they decided to invite the slaves to come and visit the camp. If they wanted to join them, they would be welcome. They would have just enough time to build some homes and get ready for winter. The homes would not be well-built but temporary homes till spring.

So the Captain, a select number of men, and a few women went to see if Jubal and his group wanted to join the camp and live a much better life. Traveling back to the fort didn't take six weeks as it had in the past. It now took only three weeks. The scouts, after getting to know the area better, found shortcuts. They finally reached the fort and greeted Jubal and his group.

Captain Jarrett meet with Jubal and his advisors, telling them what he had in mind and what they could expect. If they wished, they could come and spend the winter with them. In the spring they could decide if they would stay or go back to the fort. So they went off to themselves, and after a while, they came back and said that it sounded good. They would now tell the group and make sure they had the approval of the majority.

Everyone in the group decided to go to the camp for the winter because they were unsure of the winter at the fort. They were still scared of Sasquatch, whose attack was still fresh in their minds, and they didn't want to face him again. Also, the bears and wild cats were coming around more often. So they secured all the buildings and sheds, making sure the gate was well closed and headed toward the new camp.

They would be traveling for the better part of three weeks and going through some rough swamp all the way. Jubal was excited about getting to the new location from what he had been told. He wanted to see the waterfalland the freshwater pool in the swamp, which was unheard of.

The people at the camp knew that Jubal's group could never know about the treasures and their secret past.

They had to be treated as they were, as outsiders, always. If a person like Ruman got any idea of there being a treasure, he would not stop till he had it all. He would kill to find his way outside to get others to come back to capture it, never considering anyone else, young or old. Even those living in the camp, for the most part, didn't know that much about the pirates' treasures. The knowledge of them was given out only to the family heads. They were the ones that had a family copy of the logbook that Captain Drake Strader had begun, and they added to their copy as the history of the camp continued concerning their families.

The group was extra large, and it took a few days longer than three weeks to get to the camp. As Jubal entered, he stopped, kneeled on one knee, and read what was written on the stone. Then he smiled a big smile and said, "This is good."

It took a while before everyone could get settled, rested, and relaxed. Then the others in the camp started to bring them food, water, and rum to eat and drink. After they had finished, they were ready for bed. It was a warm, clear night, with a full moon and a little breeze, so they slept in the camp yard by firelight in tents.

The next morning everyone went to the barroom and had a good breakfast. After that Jubal had his group gathered together outside because the Captain had a few things to say. First, he wanted to know what size houses they would need to get them through the winter and how many would be staying in each house. These houses would be temporary; if they decided to stay at the camp, they would build them permanent homes like the others. "One last thing," the Captain warned "The main house by the pool, it is sacred to us. No one is to go near it or to touch it. If you do, you will be put to DEATH! Anyone with questions should ask me or Jubal only! I will give Jubal any details you need to know. Ask no one else; they will not answer you."

At this point, it was very important for the group to obey all the rules and not try to sneak around and bend them. It was most important that everyone obeys!

They got started right away on the homes, building Jubal's home first, then starting with the homes that had to be the largest. The homes went up quickly; it was the chimneys that took the most time since they were being made out of stone. They wanted the large families to build their homes close to where they wanted to live if they stayed. They would go ahead and build the chimney large enough for them and not build it again.

The other chimneys they would tear down and rebuild because they were so much smaller. Everyone was going into the swamp to get the things they needed to build the houses. It was so well organized because they had done it so many times, plus they had the extra help.

Within several weeks the houses were complete. It was late in the year and getting close to winter. Some of the people noticed how Ruman kept walking around Captain Strader's home, admiring it. He was amazed at the quality of craftsmanship in the woodwork on the house. He could only wonder what it must look like on the inside; it must be fantastic. Each day his desire grew more and more, and one day it would be a problem for him if he did not get control of it.

Ruman was not the kind of man to let things settle that excited him. This was the kind of thing that got his blood moving, making him think a lot, and that was not good.

Jubal knew what Ruman was like and noticed how he was acting lately. So he went to Captain Jarrett and reminded him about Ruman and told him what he had observed. He reminded the Captain that Ruman was the only problem he had ever had with the group, and he was a dangerous man.

Captain Jarrett thanked Jubal for coming forward and letting him know ahead of time. He said he would notify the trustees and the guards to keep a special watch on him. They were to also make notes of any unusual activities he was involved in or continued to do. After some time, Ruman had quite a list of activities he had been doing. He was a strange one.

The winter was wet and cold with sleet and ice and some snow. The ice was hard on everyone, it made it bitter cold with the wind. No one wanted to go out and cut firewood. Then the firewood started getting so low that the Captain had a large group of men go out and cut some. They had to make several trips to build up the supply again. Captain Jarrett went with them on one trip to make sure they were cutting hardwood. Some of the men were selecting softwood because it was easy to cut, but it burns up very fast. If everybody cut softwood, they would run out of firewood again and have to come back in less than half the time.

They knew that, but they were cold and wanted to get home to the warm fire, even if it was a fastburning fire. There was nothing as comfortable as sitting in their favorite chair next to a fire in the chimney, drinking coffee, and watching the fire flicker and wave as it moves upward. Felling the warmth of the fire eased every troubled thought, making them think of only pleasant loving memories and forget about what was going on, on the outside until the firewood stored up inside ran out, and they had to go out in the cold to get more.

Having to get up and put on the boots and the big coat seemed like a major chore. Fighting the cold, making two or three trips carrying firewood with frozen hands made them ready to get back to that fire.

Finally, they would get back into their chairs after getting the fire hot again and get comfortable, laid back, warm, and ready for those lovely thoughts. The wives brought a freshly brewed pot of coffee to set next to the fire to keep hot along with a section of bread and a chunk of meat to eat with beans. Now, that was the life!

Yes, the winter was rough and hard, but they got through it with several getting sick but no deaths. The days were getting a little longer and warmer now. There was still a cold chill in the air in the mornings and heavy fog frost was not unusual either.

As it was getting warmer and everyone was moving around and more active, the women were busy preparing the hides for making clothes for the men and children. The last year had proven to be hard on their clothing and buckskins. The men will be busy as usual hunting, fishing, and trapping. There will also be a group that will go to the trading post for the general store at the camp and anyone wanting any special items.

The men wanted to get several wild hogs to have for a special barbecue for their visitors. Jubal said his group did love a good barbecue, and they ate their fill. The slaves were really feeling good about the new location and how they were accepted by the white people.

The middle of April would be here in twelve days and that meant that it would be time to detail Captain Strader's House. This was not a dreaded time for the people but an exciting time. Cleaning that magnificent house and checking for repairs, just being in its presence, made you fantasize about living there. You couldn't help but think what it was like being Captain Drake Strader and living in this home. His people did indeed love him so much to give him such a fine home. To them, it was a Shrine something sacred and not to be mistreated or disrespected in any way.

It was not unusual to find people with Drake, Strade, or something similar as their first or middle name. Captain Strader, in all his years, never married. He said he never had time for anyone else; he was just too busy with his work and his people. That was his entire life.

It finally came, April 12, 1794, time to repair and clean Captain Drake Strader's house. Captain Jarrett selected women to do the cleaning, and several loyal men to do the repairs. Then there would be the guards that would closely watch over the furnishings, his personal weapons, the personal belongings around his desk, bedroom, china room, and kitchen, and the other private displays of his ventures.

The house was like a museum lost in the swamp of Goshen, North Carolina. Built from the finest wood around, wood that would last for many centuries, that made up not just the building but also the trimmings, the furniture, stairways, high ceilings, and the beautiful large doors and windows overlooking the pool and waterfall. King Solomon would have loved it for a summer home.

The work was going smoothly; the repairs were mostly on the roof and a little on the side. It looked like it would take about ten days to complete. The women were finished cleaning in about six days.

Everyone was gathered around but not too close. The rules were very strict about how close one could get. They wanted to see as much as they could inside while they were working. The doors and windows were left open when they were working to let in the fresh air.

Ruman was especially interested and was out there every day. He never got bored of hanging around, moving from door to window, to another window, and back to the other door. Some people were worried that he would try to get into the house for some reason, usually not a good one. Ruman would even go out at night and stand in the shadows for long periods, staring at the Captain's house.

What Ruman was doing was trying to figure out a time to break into the house at night because it was not securely bolted while being repaired. The moon would be full in a day or two, and about three a.m. would be a good time to catch the guard asleep. The next night the moon was almost full so Ruman decided to make his move. He was able to pick the lock on the back door and move quickly to the center chamber of the house where the armory was kept. He wanted the Captain's sword, gun, and knife. That would make him feel invincible, like a leader of men who could not be harmed.

He stole the things he wanted, locked the door, took them to his house, and hid them. He couldn't sleep, not from guilt but from thinking about how smart he was to pull it off. He thought about how he could lead a rebellion of slaves against the whites and free the slaves in the south. He would be a hero, much like Captain Drake Strader, to the slaves.

The next day the men came in to work and things went as usual. They informed the Captain that by mid- morning the next day they would be finished. So he told his trustees to give their final inspection of the house and get it ready for the bonding closure of the house till October 12, 1794.

The men went through the house and everything checked out with no problems. They never suspected that anyone would steal anything from the house.

Ruman had pulled it off, and now all he had to do was keep it hidden from everyone. He would have to somehow figure out how to get away from the camp and back to the world with them.

For sure he would have to kidnap one of the scouts that knew the way to the trading post. He would have to save food and water for the trip for both of them. He may even have to kill the scout when he got to the entrance of the swamp. He will decide that later. When he decides to make his move, it will have to be very early, before light. He will take the scout hostage late the night before, so he can make the early start the next morning.

Captain Jarrett ask Jubal if he and his group were satisfied and wanted to stay at the camp. Jubal said it sounded good to him and he would make sure the others felt the same. He came back and said everyone agreed except one, Ruman. He wanted to go back to the fort. Since he would not go back by himself though, he would stay.

The Captain said the men would get started right away tearing down the houses one at a time. They would build the new home as they wanted it, and when it was completed, tear down another, continuing until everyone, married and single, had their own home at a location they were happy with.

It was taking longer to build the homes with the families that had the most children. They were the largest homes and needed extra rooms with storage spaces and bedrooms. There were about three of those kinds of homes, and they also needed extra work with the chimney, adding more cooking arms inside the fireplace.

These three homes added another four months to the building process making it about mid-August now. These homes were being built with quality, which took time. Now the other homes would be built, moving along much smoother.

Ruman knew his time was running out, and he was going to have to make his move soon. There were only a couple of months left before they would be cleaning Captain Strader's house again. Then they would know for sure that the items were missing. He would wait as long as he could until they were ready to clean the Captain's house. That way they would be occupied preparing for the cleaning and getting everyone organized.

They would go to one of the homes that were thrown together, remove the belongings to where the owner wished, tear down the home, starting with the chimney, and take the stones to the location he chose. Then they would rebuild a stronger chimney and a better cooking fireplace.

They were moving so fast that they finished early. Instead of wasting time, they decided to go ahead and tear down Ruman's home and have it ready to start early the next morning. While they were tearing down the chimney and going through his belongings, they found the gun, sword, and knife belonging to Captain Drake Strader. The men were struck with shock and fear. They knew what this meant for Ruman.

Ruman at the time had gone on a hunting trip and would not be back till the next day or two. He thought he was in good shape and had fooled everyone. Yet, what a surprise would be waiting for him when he came home from his hunt.

The men took the three items to Captain Jarrett, and he sent for Jubal. When Jubal arrived, the Captain explained what had happened and what the law was for anyone that had done what Ruman had done. Ruman and the others had been instructed what the laws were and what the judgment against them would be. Jubal said that he agreed and that all his people agreed also.

Work on Ruman's house was stopped; he would have to live in what was left of it because the camp had no jails or prisons. He would be under guard, and he would do the needed repair on his home. He would be considered an outsider.

The next day Ruman came to camp late in the evening and was put under guard. He came back with two other men, and they were completely in shock when they found out what Ruman had done.

Time was not wasted, Captain Jarrett formed a Judicial Committee to hear the evidence the next day and invited Jubal to sit in as a guest. A Judicial Committee was to hear and see all the evidence from all eyewitnesses concerning the case. This included anything pertaining to the case that happened before the event.

It took two days to hear all the evidence against Ruman. Anyone that had anything good to say on his behalf was given time to speak. Only one spoke on his behalf, which was Jubal, and it was short. The Committee put the meeting to rest and said they would adjourn and reopen the court later with a decision.

After considering the evidence carefully, it was unanimous GUILTY! They went outside and had Ruman brought to the barroom for his plea to be read to him. It was read that he was GUILTY of THEFT and TREASON and would be thrown alive into the ALLIGATOR POOL till DEAD.

This would be carried out the next day Saturday, October 7, 1794. They would leave the camp, and it would take better than two weeks to reach the pool. The executioner would read the charges to the defendant again, and the procedure would continue. He would be thrown alive, tied and bound, into the pool with the gators. Anyone that wished to make the trip could go, but there were not very many that went, only the ones that wanted to make sure they knew the way and make sure he did not escape.

It took the group eighteen days to get to the pool. The judgment was carried out at 2:15 p.m. on Wednesday, October 25, 1794. No one knew Ruman's birth date, not even him. The gators attacked him as soon as he hit the water, so he didn't have time to really suffer at all. That was a fast way to die and a hard way to die, but it was a death that people remembered and would do everything they could to avoid.

Alligator Pool

When the group got back, they made the report that the judgment had been carried out. There would be no memorial for Ruman, and there would be no grave marker showing he was ever there.

This was the first rebellion in the camp and the first execution performed in almost one hundred years. The only mention of Ruman to be remembered would be in the logbook of Captain Drake Strader's Manual of the Ship and Camp.

Captain Jarrett right away started building the remaining homes and a school for Jubal's group, dividing it up into three groups: one for the small children, one for the middle-aged children, and the other for the adults. The small children would go to school all day and the middle-aged most of the day if not all day, depending on their workload and chores. The adults would spend about three hours a day at school and each person would complete the courses, languages, and all studies.

This would be a real challenge for Jubal and his people

because they had never been allowed to read and write. Most of them had never seen a book or pictures in a book. All they knew about the world was stories handed down over the years by their relatives about where they had lived and come from. They originally came from Africa, across the ocean, which took many months by ship, and a lot of the people died along the way. There were little food and water with terrible storms that sank some ships that were with them.

That was all they knew of the outside world. They had fresh minds that had never been filled with anything to confuse them. So once they got the basics of learning and started applying themselves, it would become very easy for them because the rest of the camp would be there to help them. Getting started would be the mountain that they all would have to climb. This would be all completely new, and anything new is scary.

They finished the houses and are just a few days away from completing the school. Jubal's group is all excited about being in their new homes. It's a dream come true for them, having and owning their own home with land for a garden.

As the group grows and begins to expand, in the future, there will be more space to build more homes. Also, some of the group will be leaving from time to time, going to the world outside. They will be trying new adventures and exploring new ways of life. As for Jubal's group, the outside does not look promising for them, being past runaway slaves.

It was now the winter again, about mid-January 1795, and it was another cold one. They finished the houses just in time for the winter. The others in the camp were busy cutting extra firewood for Jubal's group, knowing they would not have time to cut enough by themselves. They did have time to hunt, fish, and trap for food for the winter.

Jubal and a couple of his men were fishing with a net in a watery part of the swamp when Jubal pulled on a tree that a beaver had been chewing on. It broke, falling across the boat, breaking it in half, and sinking it. Jubal was injured on his right side and shoulder. One of the other men injured his left leg, but he could walk. They managed to save their fresh water and some food but lost their guns except for one. Their powder was wet, and that would take some time to dry.

They made it back to the bank where it was a little dryer and they could catch their breath. Their clothing was wet and they were cold and a long way from home. It was not midday yet, so after they got some rest they headed home. The first thing they were taught was how to navigate through the swamp, day or night. Yet, at night it is best to wait till morning, especially without a full moon.

It may take about six days on foot with injuries to get back home. The men were sore and moved slowly, doing the best they could and anxious to get home. It took them four days because they ran into a couple of hunters from the camp, so they were home in no time. The doctor checked them out and treated them, then sent them home for a lot of rest and love.

The whole camp was so excited to hear the good news that they were back and in good hands. When one person in the camp hurts, the whole camp hurts, until that person is on his feet and feeling better. That is the kind of bond that was in the camp and has always been there.

Even for the sick ones, they still had to go to school if possible, and if not, the class would be brought to them. Education was very important, and falling behind could set one back a long time. So they tried to keep on schedule with the others, which made learning so much easier.

Learning was a technique that needed feeding at a constant pace, helping the person to visualize, reason, understand, and gain knowledge of what they are being taught. If they are reading, they must see the picture of what is happening. If spelling, they must picture the word in their mind till it becomes knowledge to them. They should reason about the subject till they understand it in detail to get knowledge.

All people are different and learn differently. Some are born smart and pick up things easily while others learn by hands-on, doing it themselves. Then there are those who learn quicker by just watching someone else do it for them. No matter which way they learn, they still have to be taught and to have a teacher.

CAPTAIN JARRETT

CHAPTER SEVEN
1800s, Goshen Swamp, North Carolina

It is now April 12, 1805, and the people are getting ready to clean and repair Captain Drake Strader's house. The work should be done in six days or less because there are no major repairs, mainly cleaning. When they are finished, the trustees are sent in for a final inspection. The inspections are now very detailed, making sure everything is in place.

Cubed Browning was a negro around thirty years old with a very special talent. He was an excellent artist and sculptor and could sculpt out of wood or stone the exact likeness of an animal or man. He started out sketching on anything he could find that would hold still. When he started school, he went to the library and found two books on drawing and painting. These taught him the basics of his art and were very important, improving his work a lot. What he needed now was a master to teach him the deeper things.

His home was filled with all kinds of sculptures of different kinds of animals. When he needed anything he would go to the General Store and trade one or two of his sculptures for what he needed. He still would go out on hunting and fishing trips with the others when he had time. Everyone enjoyed his company as he was a pleasant man and never seem to get very angry.

Captain Jarrett was going to Raleigh and wanted to get a supply of the new guns and pistols he had been hearing about through the grapevine. He had other things on his mind that he was interested in also. It may not be possible but he was willing to spend the money to find out. This was something they didn't have at the camp and he was willing to give it a try. Again, time would tell.

The Captain got his things packed, taking a couple of the water buffalo to pull the wagons for the trip to Raleigh. It would be a long trip and they would be gone for a long time. The Captain took eight of his best-trained men with him because he was taking a bit of gold and silver on this trip. He had intentions of purchasing some quality goods, and they might run into trouble coming back.

He also took two women to take care of the cooking, sewing, and tending of the fires. The women always seem to help keep the men's tempers down just by being around. It put a soothing effect in the air around the camp.

These men have a lot of respect for each other anyway. It is very seldom that they have any serious disagreements. They were all brought up to think of each other as brothers. This trip would make them closer as brothers, and they would learn to give more respect to Captain Jarrett because they were a little younger.

This would be their first trip to Raleigh. They had gone to the trading post several times, and some had gone to trading posts up farther north. Yet, Raleigh was special. It was big and new with foreigners, giving them a chance to try out the languages they learned in school. Maybe they would meet some women that were foreigners and rich, who would take to them. That would be something to go home and brag about.

In the city, you could find many things to brag about. Captain Jarrett decided to send a couple of the men to the college in Raleigh for a two-week course in trapping animals the way it is done in other parts of the world. Maybe they could come back with some good ideas. The course did pay off, the men learned some new tricks. They were excited to get back home and give them a try, especially the new ideas they had for fishing.

Captain Jarrett checked out new books for the library on subjects of science, art, sculptures, and all the updated material on the school subjects and medical projects. They would take the new books, find the new points, and print them out to be used with the lessons when they were studied. The camp printing press was very handy for this kind of job. The Captain would look around for any new items that might help with the printing, mainly paper and ink and material to make books and bind them with leather.

While he was shopping, he didn't forget the main project he went for. He set aside one day just for that. He searched all over town for a respectable artist. When he thought he had found the best, a Master Alexander Roxie Boswell, who was known for paintings of Secretaries of State, Governors, Land Barons that had plantations, and even a beautiful young poor girl on the street that proved to be a most successful painting for him, all making him wealthy, the Captain went to see him.

The Captain came in unannounced, asked to speak to Master Boswell, and was told he was busy. Yet he was standing at the doorway to his office and told the man to send the Captain in.

On entering, the Captain told Mr. Boswell about his friend and his abilities, but he had never tried to paint. He wanted to purchase the things that an artist would need to do paintings on canvas, and he asked for any pointers he could add. Mr. Boswell was a down-to-earth man and was extremely impressed with the story of Cubed Browning since he was a black runaway slave. He wanted to help the boy any way he could, giving the Captain everything he needed, including some books to help him along. When the Captain left, Mr. Boswell told him to keep in touch; he wanted to keep up with the young man and help any way he could. When he needed more supplies, he should be sure to call on him. The Captain now had all the painting supplies he needed. He sent for two of his men to pick up the supplies   and take them to the wagons. He then set out to purchase some quality new guns and pistols, leather pouches, and boots.

When he finally found what he wanted, he went back to their camp and settled in for the night after a good supper. The next day about mid-morning they went to the stores to pick up the guns and other supplies. Then they headed back to Goshen Swamp where they knew they would be safe. On the trip back they would have to be on the lookout because the guns were a valued product they were carrying home.

It would be a long slow trip, but it had been exciting to see the many new things going on in the world. It was so different from the swamp with so much more to do if one had the time and money.

They were about two hours out of town when they noticed two men following them on horseback. The Captain ordered two men to walk alongside the wagons with the drivers and the other three inside the wagons. The men rode up asking if they could ride along for a spell. The Captain said a spell would be good, that they would be taking a break soon. The three were to stay hidden in the wagons while they took their break, letting the men think they knew how many there were on their trip. When they started again on their trip, the other travelers went on ahead. The Captain said that they would be hit at dark when they were asleep.

When night fell, they ate supper while the other men stayed hidden in the wagons with extra guns loaded and ready for the attack they knew was coming, but when?

After everyone had been asleep for an hour, the two men rushed in. Yelling, screaming, kicking dust, and knocking the men around, demanding they hitch up the teams of water buffalo to the wagons. After the wagons were hooked up and everyone looked safe, the other men slipped up and knocked out the two thieves. Then they took them to the nearest town and had them locked up.

From then on their trip was a safe but cautious one. They were at the entrance to Goshen Swamp before they knew it. They were home, but they still had a long way to go on boat now, fighting snakes, beaver, brush, and a bear now and then or a wild cat, while trying to keep the cargo dry and safe.

They did stop for camp one night; it was a new moon and they could not see their hands in front of them. They heard the sound of a violent attack between animals near the camp. It was a vicious fight that went on for some time. Turns out the next day it was two bears fighting. A mother bear had protected her two cubs from what must have been a big male bear. The large bear killed the mother bear, and her cubs had run up a large cypress tree for protection. They were a good size for cubs, so the team went on their way.

They finally arrive at the camp and everyone was so excited to see what was new that the Captain had brought back. Not only the Captain but the other men also had exciting things, too. The ladies were impressed with the new colors of cloth he brought back for the General Store in the camp. There were so many new items brought back they could use.

With the new guns, it meant that Jubal's group would have more guns to use when hunting now. It was like a holiday in the camp for the people. That night Captain Jarrett said they would have a cookout and dance at the barroom for everyone.

When the ladies came, they made sure they brought plenty of pies and cakes. They never ran short of rum and different kinds of spirits; that would be a hazard if they did. There were always large chunks of meat roasting over the fire ready to cut and eat.

The next morning the General Store was full of people wanting to buy and trade for the new products that were brought in from Raleigh. The new guns were handed out by the Captain to the scouts he knew were deserving of them. The first thing they did was go out and set the sights to see how far they would be accurate. They were so surprised to see that they could shoot almost twice as far. That was unheard of in that day and time.

The people in this camp were happy and satisfied. Captain Drake Strader would be well pleased to see how happy his people had become over the years and how they had grown and were educated. This was no ragtag bunch of people on the loose; they were well organized and civilized.

No one in the camp was as happy or surprised as Cubed when he saw what the Captain had brought him from Raleigh. The painting set was a dream come true; paints with different colors, a stand, and canvas to paint on. First, he had to learn on paper, when he had gotten close to perfection, then he would switch to canvas.

Before he started to do any painting, he read the section on how to mix the colors he had to get different colors. That expanded his choice of colors he could paint with. This young man could not control his excitement. He was up day and night reading and experimenting as he read. At the end of the week, he was exhausted and ready for a couple of days' rest.

Everyone could see his eagerness to learn and how fast he was applying what he was learning. His talent came out brilliantly with his new trade secret, painting! This would be what would make his name known and give him a comfortable living like he had never dreamed of. This was no fairy tale; this was real life. The future had many surprises for Cubed Browning and his abilities as an artist and sculptor.

Three and a half years later, on January 10, 1810, Cubed had become a master at the paintings he had been doing. Captain

Jarrett has decided it is time for Cubed to do the chores he has had planned for him.

First, he will have him make a large rustic picture frame to set a painting of him in to hang in the barroom and share with everyone. Then he would have a detailed sketch of Captain Rocca Lombardi done, given by his closest friends. From that Cubed would do as close a painting to the likenesses as he can. Using a large cypress rustic frame for the picture to be hung in the barroom also.

Time went by and the pictures were beautifully done and hung in the barroom. It was now in the mid part of August 1810, and time for the real challenge. They needed to get the older ones that could remember stories or the likeness of what Captain Drake Strader looked like. Then he would have Cubed sketch his likeness and do a painting with a large cypress frame. It again took several months but it was completed, with all three paintings hung on the back wall. They were hung high on the wall facing the open floor. Captain Drake Strader's picture was placed in the middle with Captain Rocca Lombardi's picture on his right side and Captain Jarrett Barlow on the left.

When the people saw the pictures unveiled, a sense of awe swept through the whole building followed by loud yelling of excitement. The people felt their loved ones were back with them, again. It was a time for celebrating and dancing, tomorrow was another day and a new year, 1811, January the first.

Almost ten years have gone by. The date was April 12, 1820, and that day they were preparing to clean and repair Captain Strader's house. Again, there are only a few repairs to be made, so it should take about five or six weeks. This year they will be doing repairs on their homes also and the other buildings in the camp. The General Store and the barroom would need special attention since they are used by so many.

There would be a select number of people to work at camp and a select number to do the hunting and fishing for the camp. Some of the women would have to cut firewood for the cooking. That meant they would have to travel some distance from the camp as firewood was getting scarce close to the camp. They didn't have to use as much hardwood as they would for heating the houses. For cooking, they could use a little more softwood to make the oven hotter quicker.

Captain Jarrett has had trees replanted where they were cut down years earlier, but they were not yet mature enough to cut. He had black oak, cedars, white oak, birch, cottonwood, poplar, cherry, plum, peach, black cherry, weeping willows, and cypress planted. He wanted a large selection growing in the swamp and spreading, giving them a good selection for building materials for furniture and dressing for the outside of their homes as well as pies. He planted a selection of cherry trees and dogwood trees around the water pool and throughout the camp. The women had already brought in different varieties of flowers and bushes that flowered, putting them throughout the camp. The Captain had sent some of his scouts out earlier to collect as many beehives as they could. While they were gone he had a carpenter build about a dozen houses with trays for the bees. There had to be a special section built to keep the queen bee in; if she decided to leave, the rest of the bees would follow.

The queen is much larger than the other bees, so they had to put her in a compartment with chambers big enough for the other bees to get in to feed her and tend to her, yet small enough that she could not get through and still lay her eggs on the outside. The rest of the box would have honey that was clean and without any eggs in it or trash from the queen. So when they pulled the rack out and cut the honey off, it would be pure honey ready to eat. Just put it into the jars you wanted to store it in, till time to eat.

The bee boxes were finished, and about a week later the scouts returned with the bees and filled the boxes. Any extras were set aside till their boxes were built. Then the boxes were spread out with a few inside the camp. Almost all were put outside in the swamp closest to the meadows. Now the problem would be bears. There is nowhere to hide honey from bears; that is their favorite treat. You just have to kill all you can in the area to keep your bees safe. The camp had been there long enough that there are not many bears left in the area.

The bear, when he gets into a honeycomb, he goes first for where the eggs are because there the young bees are hatching. This, along with the taste of the rest of the meal, delights him. The stings only bother him in his ears, nose, and eyes till he finally gives up and leaves. If the queen survives, there is a chance the hive may survive if there is enough honey left for them.

Spring is the time to pull the honey because the flowers will have been in blossom for some time and ready for the bees. The bees, in a short time, will have all the boxes filled with honey. After they collect the honey, they will leave some for the hive to rebuild on. Honey was very rare and expensive. The average hive produced around sixty pounds of honey a year and is collected twice a year, usually. There was almost no upkeep needed for the hive or box, just making sure no animals or insects invade the box and checking maybe once a month or looking in on them when walking by till around the middle of June or September to collect the honey.

Jubal and his group were very happy and satisfied with their decision to stay at the new camp. This was indeed a dream come true for them. They not only had a good education now but were able to speak in different languages. Although they still had not completed their schooling, they were close.

Cubed Browning was still improving his painting and his sculptures, and he was making money. He had traded so many things that he was asking for coins, silver, and gold for his work. He had asked Captain Jarrett for an extra storage building to store his paintings and sculptures until they could go to the trading post to sell them. The Captain told him they did have one available shed, but it needed some repairs. Do the repairs and he could use it.

The Captain decided to make a quick trip to Raleigh; he was interested in seeing Master Alexander Roxie Boswell. He would be going the next morning with just two men, one wagon, and one dog. When daylight came they were on their way with the water buffalo pulling the boat down the swamp. This trip would not be as long as usual because it would go faster with only one wagon.

When they got to Raleigh, the Captain met with Mr. Boswell. They talked for over two hours about Cubed Browning and his work. Mr. Boswell said that he had a studio with an extra adjoining room that he was not using. If Cubed wanted to, he could set up shop with him and sell his paintings and his sculptures. If anyone asked, he would say that he was Boswell's slave. They would work out the details later if he chose to go along with the idea. The Captain thought he would accept the idea.

The Captain left the next morning and headed for home. The dog was really handy and never let anyone get too close to their camp, day or night. The Captain said the dog would go with them in the future, adding an extra guard.

They were back home, having had a good trip and no problems. They were welcomed back by everyone but no gifts! What a letdown! There was good news for only one person if he accepted it. Captain Jarrett spent no time going to see Cubed and telling him what Mr. Boswell had suggested.

Cubed listened intently to what the Captain had to say and was overjoyed at the news. He said this was his first real chance to display his art to people with real class. The Captain told him he could not take anything that showed the camp's setting without his approval first. Nothing displaying the camp in the swamp was allowed outside the camp. He had to completely forget his time in the swamp and make up another story about where he got the products for his sculptures and paintings.

He collected all his belongings along with his paints, art, and sculptures, and he was off with several scouts for Raleigh. They made it to Raleigh and Mr. Boswell helped Cubed set up in the studio on a popular street in Raleigh. Mr. Boswell had rented a small room upstairs in the studio for Cubed to live in and manage the studio. As customers came in, they were very excited about the sculptures Cubed had done. Never had they seen such detail of the animals carved out of a cypress tree stump. They were buying sculptures faster than Cubed could replace them. He didn't have time to do any painting at the time, just when he needed a break from carving. He was working all day and up into the night. To him, it was not work because he was enjoying himself so much.

He had never dreamed of having the money he was making and didn't know how he would spend it; he would just save it. He spoke to Mr. Boswell about his problem.

Mr. Boswell said that he put his money into the bank and when he needed cash he would draw out what he needed. Cubed thought that was a good idea, so he and Mr. Boswell went to the bank and opened up an account under his business name, Browning's Art and Sculptures. Now he had to learn about taxes and books. He was a businessman now! The day was Tuesday, August 28, 1821.

A year later a strong hurricane hit the central part of North Carolina with strong winds that destroyed trees and buildings. It hit the campsite with high winds and rising waters. The buildings were strong and stood up against the wind, but the rain was coming from everywhere. Water came inside the buildings about two feet high; flooding was everywhere.

The hurricane struck the camp about midafternoon September 27, 1822, and continued till late into the night. The night and next day were miserable for the people of the camp. The Captain said the only thing the people could do was to make themselves comfortable as best they could and wait for the water to go down: maybe in a day, maybe two. They were warned to be careful of the water they drank and get it from the spring at the top of the waterfall because it should be fresh there.

It took two days for the swamp water to go down to normal, and a lot of the food had spoiled. Conditions were made worse when people started getting sick. It was especially hard on the elderly and the very weak and sickly. It wasn't long before people started dying, more and more as time went on. Food was scarce and living conditions were hard; no one could get comfortable.

The doctors were afraid that cholera would set in and make things worse.

Captain Jarrett sent out scouts and others to get needed meat and fish for the camp. Repair of the camp could wait till everyone got their health back. The first thing was to get the mud out of the homes and dried out after the food was brought in.

Getting the camp back into good condition was not going to be an easy job. It would be a long, drawnout ordeal, that would affect every man, woman, and child of every size. It would take years for the swamp to recover. The trail to the trading post through the swamp would have to be cleared for travel. The water buffalo would come in handy for this kind of work. No doubt many trees had blown over the swamp runs where they would be traveling through.

They had to be careful how they cleared the path through the water. It had to be hidden underwater as much as possible. If it showed that someone had cut a trail, that would be like leading them to the camp. Some of the ends would have to show burns where maybe lighting had struck, instead of where an ax had cut, having a mossy covering with a bush there to hide the evidence. These men were using every trick in the book to hide their camp. It took about four years to get things back to normal again. They lost a lot of their friends from the hurricane.

It was now December 5, 1826, and this was the worst thing that had happened to the people at the camp in the 121 years that they had been in North Carolina. They had stood up against the British, bounty hunters, Indians, swamp beasts, freezing winters, hot summers, droughts, and now hurricanes. The hurricane proved to be the worst and deadliest of all the hazards that had struck the people.

CAPTAIN JASPER STANDISH

CHAPTER EIGHT
Goshen Swamp and the Outside World

On Tuesday, April 18, 1837, Captain Jarrett Barlow died at the age of 85. Before his death, he appointed Logan's great-grandson as his successor. Captain Jasper William Standish was to lead the camp faithfully as all the other Captains had done, becoming the fourth Captain to advise and command the camp. He was well qualified, having completed all the classes and languages, graduating at the top of his class, and going to top colleges in the outside world also.

He was not one to see anyone held back from their desires but wanted to help everyone excel. He felt the mind should never be held back but should expand to its limits. He would expand the school, the library, and anything else to help the students learn. Cubed Browning had done great things with the subject of art for the school and still came by from time to time to add more.

Again, it is time to clean Captain Drake Strader's house and make any repairs. There are still many repairs to be made from the hurricane from years back. Even in the swamp, many trees are leaning from the strong winds. The hurricane didn't seem to bother any of the animals except the very young, but the beaver dams were damaged from the high waters.

Yes, the hurricane had loosened a lot of boards on the old house but it had been well kept. Being two and one-half stories high made it a good target for the hurricane. Fifteen years since the hurricane, and it seemed like yesterday. Many still remembered that afternoon and evening. The anxieties, fear and troublesome thoughts the people had during the hurricane were hard for them to get over. It went on and on as if it would never stop. The houses were built strong, which was what supported the people.

Captain Standish wanted everyone to do repairs on their homes also, inside and out, giving their homes a complete sterilizing on the inside with soapy, boiling water. Sickness had been up the past few months, so he wanted to clean all the areas he could.

Animal life was getting plentiful again, especially around the garden areas. Traps were being set, catching quite a few raccoons, opossums, and even a wild cat. Deer came in the garden often but were more cautious. With the new long guns the guards had, on a full moon they had shot a deer now and then in the garden. With the spring coming and some of the garden getting ready, the Captain was thinking about putting an extra guard station high above the ground in the middle of the garden and putting a guard on duty to kill the extra game that was coming in at night, especially the deer, and giving him an extra gun so he wouldn't have to reload. It would not be surprising if a bear or two were to start coming around this time of year. It was mating season, and they were known to roam at that time.

Fishing was still good in the swamp, and that was one thing that the women can do right there at the camp. They could go out to the water hole, throw in their hook, and after a while, they have a fish. They always took little scraps that the fish would eat and threw them to the fish to keep the fishing hole well feed. That way they would always have fish to catch.

The men did the same thing when they found a good fishing hole. They took a small sack, put cornmeal into it, and tying it off to a tree limb, let it hang in the water to let the fish suck on it. When they came back later, there would be several fish. They would refill the bag with fresh cornmeal or other ingredients that may be helpful.

The hunters did the same thing with ears of corn and salt at a certain location that the deer travel often to keep them coming. It is a method that has been used for centuries and is very effective. Why do stores have sales! Captain Standish was very interested in the trading posts in the surrounding areas, the plantations and farms,   and what was happening around Goshen Swamp and its growth. He wanted to get maps of the area, They needed to know more about their surroundings. So he sent out scouts in all directions with a mission to gather information and make drawings of what was going on around them, for him.

After a few months, the scouts reported back with reports that there were two counties they were concerned with: Duplin and Wayne Counties. Just to the northwest were several plantations owned by the Loftins, Williamses, Cobbs, Peeles, Robertses, and Kornegays. Also, there was a large farm owned by a free negro, who owned his own slaves with several hundred acres. This man, for a negro, had a lot of respect from the people in Wayne County. He treated his slaves with respect and never had any problems with them. His name was Adam Winn.

The Robertses and Kornegays were located mostly in Duplin County. That is where the entrance to the Goshen Swamp was located and the hardest to find.

The drawings showed the homes of the plantation owners and the size of their wealth. Their land and crops were of great size, with many different crops and storage buildings. The Captain was quite impressed with the outside world but said it was nothing compared to the tranquility and peacefulness of the camp. It was its own little paradise, set aside to its own place.

The drawing showed that in the future there would be a railroad going through the county and that did interest the Captain. He was thinking of a way to ship their products up north and get a better price for them. He already knew of places where he went to school that would be good buyers. If more places were needed, he would send a couple of men to the city to search out other buyers.

They would keep an eye on the progress of the railroad because it would be a long time before it came through. As soon as they knew when, they would purchase a small section of property for a store to use to ship their supplies from and to receive supplies. According to the map, the railroad is only going to be twelve to fifteen miles from the swamp entrance.

Now they just have to wait and see. On July 21, 1840, the railroad is complete in Mount Olive, and they have a train depot on Center Street. The railroad company is the Wilmington and Weldon Railroad Lines, and at the time was in fact the longest railroad in the world.

The Captain saw a chance to get ahead of the game here and not be so obvious about setting up a store in Mount Olive. He wanted to go out about two thousand feet at least from the train depot and build a store for shipping supplies to Wilmington N.C. on the train and to put on a boat to ship up north. Turns out the land that a large part of Mount Olive is built on, including part of Main Street, is owned by Adam Winn. So they have to buy land from Mr. Winn the same as the railroad and the town did. Adam Winn was making himself quite a bit of money off the railroad.

The train coming through Wayne and Duplin Counties was big news at the time; it meant growth and prosperity.

Everywhere the railroad went, towns went up, and people came from all over to make them grow.

Captain Jasper Standish set out to build a storage building for the supplies. In a few weeks, it was finished with a small dock for loading and unloading. Right away they started bringing in furs and other supplies they wanted to sell. Some of Cubed Browning's students were sending copies of the paintings and sculptures they had completed and felt were their best. Everyone was very excited about this adventure.

Jubal and his group were more excited than anyone else because this was their first time reaching out to the outside world. They had a very unique style of art in paintings and sculptures. They wanted to see how the north would accept this style of art.

Captain Standish had already gone up north and made ready for the sales on a trial basis. If things went well, that would determine the number of purchases for the next sale. Everyone was busy preparing for the next sale: busy hunting, painting, doing sculptures, and trying to create an outstanding new look.

Jubal's group had grown from twenty-eight adults and four children to around 221 persons overall. The biggest reason for the growth was that they were runaway slaves and could not go back to the world. Even their children would not be allowed back into the world without legal papers from someone on the outside. The group overall had risen to above nine hundred and would be over a thousand, but so many had chosen to go live in the world outside, yet many had also returned.

The swamp still had its mysterious ways about it; Sasquatch was still seen in many parts of the swamp. No one tried to confront him or interfere with his business. They found a place to conceal themselves until he moved on, well out of the way. Pretty much the same with bears, unless they had the advantage and wanted the meat and skin. Bear skins were very much needed for coats and covers for sleep and to keep warm in the winter. Their meat lasted a long time as there was so much of it. In the winter the meat lasted much longer because of the cold weather. A man doesn't have to go out and hunt as often in the winter when he has killed a bear or a large deer.

Word came in that their products were selling and selling fast. They needed as much and as fast as they could send them of what they had on supply. Everyone was so excited, they had another party at the barroom, celebrating their good blessings. This meant that they could now send their inferior products, the ones they were scared to send at first. They started getting things ready for shipping, and in a few days, they had another shipment ready to go. The extra money would be sent to them in gold, and they would just add it to their treasure chests. Each person's family head had a treasure chest going back to the pirate days that the family depended on for education and medical use. Every chance members of the family had to add gold to the chest they did because they had little use for money in the camp. When a job was done it was usually done in trade.

The Captain had a few men take the products to the train depot to be shipped to Wilmington, N.C. to ship to the north. Then they would wait to hear how well they sold and when they would want more. Hopefully, it would be a steady business for everyone.

Captain Jasper Standish was a man much like his great uncle Luka: strong, active, and very smart. He had a wife named Kayla and two sons, one was named Marty and he was twenty years old. The other was Jay, and he was nineteen years old. Jasper saw a lot of good qualities in both of his sons but especially in Marty, even as a young man. Kayla was wise and very loving and attractive, supporting and working with the boys. They would have liked to maybe have a couple more children if things continued to go well. The Captain at this time was around forty-four years old; his wife was thirty-eight.

Time was going by, and it was November 24, 1842, and time to clean up Captain Strader's house again. It shouldn't take very long, as everything was in good repair. They had their standard party as usual at the barroom, which everyone looked forward to.

They got another gold shipment from the merchants up north as well as a list of products wanted as soon as possible. They added new requests, hoping that they could fill those orders also. The Captain got the people together and talked it over. The ones with more skills wanted to talk it over.

They came back and decided they could build what they asked for but would need some pictures. So the Captain requested drawings of what they wanted. Soon the drawings came in, and after looking them over, they figured out a simpler way to build the objects, and they would work just as well. By being built out of cypress wood they would be strong, durable, and last a long time without worry about bending, splitting, or rotting. Cypress wood was wood that lasted for many years to come.

The people were setting up assembly lines to make the most popular products and fill the storage houses. They found time to do other things and were getting restless, so Captain Standish sent a couple of wise, outstanding men up north to cities near the ones buying their products and offered them the products also. The men came back with another large order to be filled. The amazing thing was the swamp was plenty big and had more than enough game.

Things were going so well, and they had so much gold dust coming in each month, the people were at a loss as to what to do. They just kept saving, never wondering about the future.

Now, Jubal had plenty on his mind about the money his group of people had collected. He counted it up and there was enough money to pay for the freedom of the twenty-eight people that had fled the plantations. He asked Captain Standish if he would take the $28,000.00 and go to the plantations in South Carolina to try to buy their freedom. Captain Standish said without hesitation, "It would be an honor and a privilege, sir."

After receiving a letter from each person asking for their freedom in their own handwriting, with the name and location of the Master and Plantation, he left at daylight for South Carolina wasting no time and not even looking back.

He would make sure to bargain for the best price for each slave since they had no plans to return. He felt sure he would not have to pay a thousand dollars a head for their freedom. The Captain was right, the only one who had to pay a thousand dollars was Jubal, his Master would not give an inch because he was a man filled with hatred, bitterness, and anger. He said if he ever saw Jubal again, he would boil him alive, then burn what was left to ashes.

The only reason he gave him his freedom was because of his greed for the thousand dollars.

The Captain decided it might be smart to stop in Charleston, South Carolina, and while he was in town, check with a respectable lawyer to find out what the laws were concerning free slaves in South Carolina. There were many laws concerning freed slaves and their rights and how they could lose their freedom as free slaves, going back to being slaves the same as before. The captain asked for copies of those laws to bring back with him. While returning, he decided to stop in Raleigh and do the same, checking with his lawyer. He found North Carolina was much the same but not near as bad as South Carolina. It was important to always report to the county tax office each year. They realized then if they went into the world and tried to live on the outside, they would have to start paying taxes and reporting everything to the government.

When Jubal heard that and read what the laws were about freed slaves, he then compared that to what he had in Goshen Swamp and said, "No. All I wanted was the paper saying I was a free man, that's all. I didn't care what it cost; a thousand dollars was cheap."

The rest of the group felt the same as Jubal did and never wanted to leave. They could now give papers to their children saying they were free, and if they wanted to leave and live in the world, they would have that choice. The pull to the outside world would be strong and tempting, making the dangers seem to be very little of a problem for a man with an education.

Eleven years went by, and that little train depot turned into a little bit of a town called Mount Olive, and they put an updated train depot and a Post Office in town. Giden Roberts was the town's first Post Master and their first doctor. He bought some land on what became Main Street and sold it to anyone who wanted to start a business. If they couldn't pay, he gave them the land till they could, as long as they started a business. He and others were given credit for starting the town but Giden Roberts is credited as its founder because he helped so many start businesses. Giden Roberts was a surgeon for the Confederacy during the War for two years.

The railroad was quite busy these days with the talk of Civil War as strong as it was. The north was complaining about slavery and yet had four states that had slaves, never freeing their slaves in one state until months after the Civil War ended. It was the shame of the north for a long time after the War, till it was finally put to an end. That state is the state of Delaware.

The southern states felt they had the right to continue to have their slaves but any new states should not. The South had slaves for hundreds of years. This issue was a problem in the outside world, but in the camp, everyone was looked at as the same. There had never been any problem with Jubal's people and the camp people because they were all Swamp People. What one had they all had, so everyone shared. It was like greed and racism were lost words.

On Tuesday, August 23, 1859, a beautiful day for North Carolina, the young boys in the countryside were going swimming, fishing, or both after their chores. The boys planned on meeting at the meal pond where they grind meal from corn and other crops. There was a water wheel, that turned the millstone that ground the corn to meal. The water came from a lake they fish and swim in every chance they get. There was not a kid for miles that could not swim.

The people at the camp were looking forward to going to Mount Olive as well as the trading post. Soldiers were coming into town and setting up a command post out behind the train depot. It looked like about a company of Union soldiers, but these are not just soldiers, they were the Calvary on horseback. The Captain did not give any reason why they were there or how long they would be there. It looked like a market for some rum or spirits.

People say they made patrols up and down the tracks through town and around the countryside and patrolled a lot at the trading post, asking a lot of questions about any strangers, unusual people, or anyone doing anything strange lately.

Captain Standish thought it might be a good idea if they bought three sets of horses and three large wagons to carry their goods to the depot and stop using the water buffalo and the wagons they had.

Then they would tell the farmers that they are free to use the animals and wagons at no charge till the camp needed them again, which was only a few days out of the month to carry and pick up their supplies at the depot. All they had to do was take care of them and feed them for use. The wagons and animals would have the camp's brand on them.

The next day, two of the men went out and found a farmer that had just what they needed, and they paid him a handsome price for all. He was very pleased with the price. Then, when they told him what the plan was and he realized he didn't have to go out looking for more animals and wagons, he was more than excited. He was then wondering if all this was legal or not, but they assured him it was legal.

Everything was set now, and the horses and wagons were not too far from the swamp entrance when they would be ready. They would let the farmer know a couple of days early when they would need the horses and wagons. That would give him time to prepare.

After making several trips to the depot shipping products to the markets up north, the farmer was well satisfied with the arrangement. His crops were taken care of, and he was well compensated for his horses and wagons. If the horses needed extra attention or the wagons needed extra work done on them, the men paid him for the extra expense for the repair, to make sure everything was always ready to go.

They wanted him to always maintain good upkeep on the horses and the wagons. He took it upon himself to buy an extra horse and an extra wagon to keep on hand in case of a breakdown or a sick horse. The men offered to pay him extra to help out, but he said they were giving more than enough with the extra money for the upkeep.

The men informed him when they would be needing the horses and wagons for a couple of days again. As usual, they would be by about mid-morning.

They came by as planned, then went to the swamp entrance and there loaded everything onto the wagons.

Then they headed out for the train depot to ship out their goods for another payday.

This time they were greeted by Union soldiers asking questions, Who they were? Where they were from? What they were shipping and to where? How long they had lived there? They were interested in the guns they carried since they were the newest models.

Who were they?

They told them they were hunters and trappers trying to make a simple living. They had a large family that helped them prepare the hides and other products.

Where were they from?

They told them they lived down by the swamp. When asked where, they said about fifteen miles down past Beautancus Trading Post close to the Goshen Swamp entrance. The soldier settled for that since he was not familiar with the area.

What were they shipping and to where?

Rather than try to explain, they showed the lieutenant the shipping manifest and he still was not satisfied.

So he opened some of the crates and showed him.

How long had they lived there?

The men explained that they had lived there all their lives. He then questioned each of the eight men about their families, and how they made their livings. He was finally satisfied with their answers.

Where did they get the new model guns?

They told him that one of their buyers in Massachusetts had connections with a gunmaker in Philadelphia. When a new model came out that was outstanding, he would send him a copy. He in turn would send it to them, and if it was exceptional, they would send in an order. That is why they have the new models and no one else, and they had no intentions of ever selling guns to anyone. They have never done it in the past and didn't intend to; they didn't need the money that bad.

The lieutenant was completely satisfied with their answers and was impressed with their mannerism and education. As he questioned them, he observed the quality of their answers and the manner of their answers.

This was no ordinary group of farmers. He wanted to find out more about this group.

First, the lieutenant wanted to travel to the trading post in Beautancus and see what he could find out about these swamp people. The people didn't have much to say except the people were good people: honest, traded good, and had been around forever. No one knew where they actually came from or where they lived. The story goes that they live deep in the swamp, so deep no one can go in and come out alive. Everyone knows Goshen Swamp is not a place to go into very far unless you have a guide that has been there many times, and he will go just so far because of the stories of the swamp monsters and of fishermen who say they have seen Sasquatch in those swamps. Not only that but the size of the bears is unbelievable and vicious.

The lieutenant was very confused. If the stories of the people living deep in Goshen Swamp were true, how did they get their education? The managers at the trading post said the people would come in and serve as translators for them in several languages often because they often had foreigners traveling through, stopping to trade and getting information for their trip. The lieutenant was now really confused that they knew several languages fluently. This needed investigating!

The lieutenant went back to his camp and made his report to the captain, the captain agreed with him. The lieutenant would investigate further, making sure this was not a southern build-up for an uprising against the North. The lieutenant started investigating the farms around the trading post, questioning them to see if they thought they were a suspicious kind of people. The farmers thought the yanks were looking for trouble for the swamp people and told them so. The lieutenant gave up questioning the farmers just before he got to the farmer's house that had the horses and wagons. He went back, making a report to the captain that most of the farmers were in on whatever the men had planned.

When the men got back, they made their report to Captain Standish who was upset that Union soldiers were now getting involved with his people. This could lead to nothing but trouble. They would have to put off going to town as long as possible a year if possible. They should have no contact with the Union, even if they come into the swamp.

"Let them come till they give up like the British, and if they get to the fort, that will be fine also. We will go back and clean up anything that looks like anyone has been there recently, leaving the gate open and letting the animals in to disrupt the area," the Captain declared.

The fort did not need much clearing out, just some ashes from the pit and some fireplaces but not much trash. The animals, in a few days, would make it look like it was unused for months or years. The animals would move in very quickly and take over. The Captain said he was not going to let a company of Union soldiers spoil what they had kept a secret for 150 years. He would let them travel one week into Goshen Swamp after leaving the fort, and if they were headed toward the camp, he would set up ambushes and destroy them.

The Captain sat down with his advisors and went over his plan, and they agreed. Then they sent out scouts to decide where to set up the ambushes and how many ambushes may be needed.

They also set up the cannons as was done before as a last standoff if needed. They were prepared as the other Captains in the past had been, and they would fight to the death. Each man, from their forefathers the Pirates, had been taught how to fight, using all the tricks of hand-to-hand combat that the Pirates knew. Using the knife with skill was a gift to them. Each man had always been a deadly weapon with his hands if the need ever occurred. The men knew that the use of deadly force would raise suspicion as to who they were, so they tried to avoid it.

Captain Standish now had his plan in place and his scouts working on traps in case anyone went past the last marker. They devised new kinds of traps that spring up from under the water, destroying the boats and usually stopping travel by water. These new traps were set to kill and stop.

This lieutenant was ambitious and desired to be a general someday. He wanted to make headlines out of every patrol he went on. That is why his Captain let him make a fool of himself, keeping his reports to himself. If anything comes of it, he will then send off the reports, saving his future and the lieutenant's future.

The lieutenant wanted to travel along Goshen Swamp a few miles down from Beautancus and look for the entrance. He already spent seven months working on this project and was not about to give up now. About mid- morning they found what they believed to be the entrance to Goshen Swamp that the men have been using.

Entrance To Goshen Swamp

Yes, it was the entrance to Goshen Swamp. Now, the order was given to march their horses into the swamp and follow the run of the swamp as far as they have been ordered. The watery mucky mess reached the top of the saddles; some of the men couldn't swim and were scared to death they would fall off their horses. The horses were not at ease, and suddenly there was a burst of several rounds of gunfire. Right away the lieutenant rushed back to where the smoke was and wanted to know what was going on. The private points next to his horse, and there lay a water moccasin shot to hell. He told the lieutenant, "No snake is going to get my horse and make me walk in this mucky, messy slime."

They continued and the water began to get a little shallower, but the yellow flies, mosquitoes, and other insects were eating them alive. They were covered with welts all over their bodies, and it was so hot they could hardly breathe. Everywhere they looked were snakes and all kinds of wild animals getting closer to them and the horses. They seemed more curious than anything, sniffing the air to get a smell of them. Now and then a badger or a wild bore would attempt to charge at them. The lieutenant decided to turn back; it would be dark by the time they got back if they were not careful.

They made their turn and headed back. It was a straight shot if they followed the run of the swamp, so they had no problem. They knew they had to have a lot of men and a lot of boats and people who knew the swamp if they were to find the swamp people. They might as well give up before they tried it again; there was no hope without someone who knew the way and that would not happen.

The lieutenant went back, making his report and deciding against going back into Goshen Swamp again without someone as a guide. No one in the counties around Mount Olive, for any amount of money, would work with the Union forces. They knew now they were out to make trouble for the swamp people who had never made problems for anyone but always helped their neighbors. They began putting more pressure on the people in the town and the counties for information about where they were located, but no one knew no one had ever gotten close enough to them to ask.

One day the lieutenant was making his rounds at one of the trading posts at Beautancus and noticed a picture, an old picture, hanging on the wall. He asked about the picture and how old it was. The manager said it was a little less than a hundred, maybe a little over ninety, years old.

"Why did they put up a picture of a fight?" asked the lieutenant."

"Because back then fights were common. These men were beaten so badly, they didn't want it to happen again, three men almost killed five very large men. The five brutes wanted to mess with their women," answered the manager. The story goes, the men fought as men have never fought before, the big men never had a chance. They were beaten and torn apart limb from limb like a bear had gotten hold of them. Their throats were ripped open but with bare hands, these men were trained for hand-to-hand combat against anyone. This picture was put here as a warning not to mess with the swamp people almost a hundred years ago, and it still goes as far as we are concerned. They mess with no one and no one messes with them. They are always helpful and kind, giving to the poor and the ones in need."

Right then the lieutenant was thinking, we are going to start a fight when we see those young men in town again. He was patiently waiting for the young men to show up again in town but couldn't understand why they had been gone for over eight months, never showing up.

Over a year later, on Monday, October 1, 1860, supplies were getting very low on everything. The Captain says it is time to ship out the products and pick up the supplies they need. He will send the same eight men he sent before, if they are questioned they will know what to say. If there is no problem they will send another load of products out right away.

They let the farmer know right away that they will be coming soon to get the horses and wagons. They leave as soon as they can, making their way down the swamp, finally making it to the entrance, and going to the farmer's to get the horses and the wagons. It doesn't take long to get back to the swamp to load the products and get on their way. The trip to Mount Olive is a smooth ride, and the wagons are in good shape.

They finally reach the train depot and unload their products so they are ready when the train arrives. The paperwork goes as scheduled, and the men are ready to pick up their supplies. Four of the men take two of the wagons to the outskirts of town and wait for the other four to get the supplies in town. They have gotten the supplies, and start on their way out of town, but as they are leaving town, they meet the lieutenant coming back from a patrol. He is some kind of happy to see these boys. He has already picked out three of his best hand-to- hand combat fighters to pick fights with these men.

These men, in their training, are taught never to show their skills unless it is to protect a family member or themselves from death. Otherwise, they use the defense method of their training. The three men got off their horses went over and pushed and pulled three men off the wagon, throwing them into the dirt. They stood laughing with the rest of the company of soldiers. The swamp men walked over together, looked at the men, and waited for their next move. The soldiers rushed, swinging at the air and trying to bully their way in as the men stepped aside, making them look like fools. They got mad, rushed again, and fell in the dirt, being kicked by the men as they went by. That was the last straw. They walked up slowly and reached out to grab the men. When they did, the men grabbed their hands turned them around bending them back. This put them into such agony they could do nothing but beg to be let go.

Now the company was laughing at them. Even the lieutenant was very impressed at the show they gave. He asked if they would be willing to teach his men those tricks. They told him all it took was patience, leverage, and self-control. They told the lieutenant that if he would back off and let them come to town with no hassle, they would teach his men. He thought about it and decided this would be a good way to get to know the men and more about them, so he agreed.

Right away, the eight men started showing the soldiers defensive moves, and after a week the whole platoon had learned the moves and were practicing every day. The lieutenant then wanted them to teach his men offensive moves, but they told him all they were taught was defense. That was all they would ever need, and to keep a cool head. The officer didn't believe a word of it; he knew these men were a deadly force with their hands. He just didn't know how to get them to show him. After seeing the picture and hearing the stories that the other people were telling about what their great-grandparents witnessed about the violence, for some reason he just knew this training was handed down year after year for over a hundred years. He wanted that training for his men, so they would be the best.

He didn't know how yet, but he was going to get one of those men to give him that training. He would need to get closer to the eight men, and if that didn't work, he would have to use force somehow.

The swamp men got on their wagons and headed back to the swamp to report to the Captain what had taken place. The Captain said the lieutenant was not finished and to be cautious of him; he was a weasel of a man and not to be trusted with your life or your friend's life. They got another load of products ready to send to the railroad depot for the North.

When they got to the depot they had unloaded their products that were crated for the train. The depot master said the train would not be in until the next morning and that their products would be fine on the dock till then. The men walked around back and noticed that the Union soldiers were gone. They asked the depot master where the soldiers were. He was shocked, saying, "You haven't heard? The South has declared War on the Union.

Yesterday, at sunrise at Charleston, South Carolina, southern forces fired on Fort Sumter, starting a war between the states using militia."

The men were excited that the soldiers were gone, most likely for a long time, if not for good. They could start shipping their products on schedule again. They picked up some more supplies and headed back to the swamp to report back to the Captain and bring back a copy of the newspaper that told of the news about the war and what else was going on around the area.

Seemed like everyone was glad to see the company of soldiers leave; two hundred extra soldiers in town over doubled the number of people in town. The money was good, but the trouble and bullying they caused were not worth it.

When the men got to camp and made their report to Captain Jasper Standish, he said he was not surprised at all. This problem had been brewing for ten years or longer and getting hotter as time got closer. "It started yesterday, and I think things will be getting back to normal, but next year or later you can look for a blockade of the waterways. Goods leaving the South will be blocked by the northern Navy."

Captain Standish wanted to send the last of the products they had to the train depot to be sent to the North. This may be their last chance for a while, you never know. His two boys, with the other six, loaded everything they could and headed for Mount Olive.

When they reached the train depot they unloaded their

freight on the loading dock and got their paperwork. They then decided to go and get supplies. Suddenly, when they looked up they saw the Cavalry riding into town. The lieutenant came up on his horse to Marty and his men, then informed him that he and his men and their horses and wagons were now property owned by the Confederate States of America. They were then taken to the back of the depot and instructed where to put their horses and wagons, while under careful guard. They were then ordered to help set up tents and do other chores any private would do.

The soldiers continued going around town and the countryside in the counties collecting all the young men and any volunteers they could get to help support the war effort.

After collecting men, horses, supplies, and anything else they could use from the town of Mount Olive and the surrounding counties, they left, leaving the community stripped-down with almost nothing to survive on. These people were hardy, and they would survive. Neighbors from far away counties heard of their problem and came to their rescue, giving them extras that they had. This helped them get restocked, and by the next spring they would be back close to normal.

When Captain Standish found out what had happened to his sons and the other men, he collected 450 men and went to Mount Olive. They all were fully armed and packed for a long journey if necessary.

When they hit town the people had no idea what to expect, but they knew one thing for sure, these men were the swamp people. They had no idea there were so many of them. Their home must be some kind of a large dwelling place in the swamp. When they got their information as to what had happened, they lined up in formations. Then they marched out of town in the direction the Cavalry had gone. They continued, as usual, shipping supplies and products North and purchasing extra guns just in case. The next year things moved well at first, but then it got slower, then slower, and then came to a complete stop. On occasion, you could risk a shipment up North, and you had a 35% chance it would get through. The Captain tried it a couple of times, and they got through. Getting their payment back was just as risky, but they were blessed there also, and both payments came through.

THE CIVIL WAR
MARTY & JAY STANDISH

CHAPTER NINE
Fighting With The Confederacy

It is Tuesday, May 28, 1861, and the Captain of the cavalry is in a rush to get to the Lee Training Camp at Richmond, Virginia. General Lee needs as many cavalry riders as possible, trained for combat or not. They are in a forced march and plan to reach Richmond in about a month. Then they will be assigned to a regiment of around eight hundred men to start a fast training session.

Lieutenant Daniel Bakersfield is from the hills of Tennessee and loves horses, riding, and fighting. He is really glad to have the swamp men with his company. The first thing he does is have them assigned to their own squad with two other men; a squad is made up of 10 men. He then has Marty moved up to the rank of private first class, putting him in charge.

On their first day, they do tryouts for riding horses at different speeds and how well they can stay on. The swamp men didn't do very well with this because they hadn't been around horses much. The next day they were shown how to fight with their swords and knives; this they knew very, very well. Their instructors could not believe the moves these men could make with their swords. These were moves that were never discussed at West Point or any other schools because they got their skills from their pirate ancestors.

Then the instructors were going to show them the proper way to handle the knife and use it in hand-to-hand combat. To demonstrate, he asked Jay to come out and take away his knife. Before he knew it he was on the ground with his knife at his throat. He humbly got up and asked, "What kind of a move was that? I have never seen that before."

Jay gave him his knife and said, "My father taught me that to protect me." The instructors realized that almost all the men in this squad were exceptional in hand-to-hand combat and were fearless fighters.

They recommended that each of these men be promoted to private first class and that Marty and Jay move up to corporal right away. These men were no ragtag bunch. They were educated and skilled. That was what the Confederacy needed most at the moment was leaders. Reports of these men would go to the top, straight to General Lee, to see what to do with them, especially when they found out from Lieutenant Daniel Bakersfield that they knew several languages.

The next day, instead of taking training with the rest of the men, they were brought into a tent and given tests of their IQs.

They were tested almost all day. Then they were given personal questionnaires about themselves as individuals and about the schools and colleges they went to.

Two days later they were brought to the Corp office, which is the head of the whole operation, and stood before General Benson Weaver. He advised them that they had scored very high on the tests and that their scores were sent directly to General Lee, asking him what to do with them. There was one problem. Although they did have ambush training, they had no military schooling and would have to learn as they go.

Captain Jasper Standish was still on the march looking for his men and his sons. He was headed in the right direction, but travel was slow. They did manage to buy a few horses, about a dozen along the way, so he sent a dozen scouts ahead to find out what they could. They would travel to Richmond before finding out that the men had been given their own companies of men to command and had left to meet General Lee at Manassas Junction. So they returned, heading back to report the news to Captain Standish.

When Captain Standish got the report, he just fell to the ground and wept like a baby. He had lost all his strength. They were next to a well-watered stream so they set up camp for a couple of days. While they had set up camp, a company of Confederate soldiers, around two hundred men, came by headed for Richmond. They stopped and asked if any wanted to join up with them. The Captain said anyone that wanted to could go, but no one wanted to go, so the soldiers went their way with no problems.

It was still morning, and the Captain said that it was time to head back home. There was nothing more they could do now, the men were scattered everywhere. So they headed back home to tell the bad news to the families.

After talking with the general, the men knew they had to learn how to ride a horse. They asked for a horse to use, but they were all being used with none to spare. They would have to learn on the job how to stay on the horse. The next day they were being taught leadership and how to deal with men of all kinds. Discipline was very important in the military, and they learned to never give in to a recruit to any degree.

On July 21, 1861, word has come in from General Lee to send every available man to his location as soon as possible for a major battle with the Union forces. The location will be near Manassas Junction, Virginia.

The eight men have been given the rank of captain and put in charge of a company of two hundred men each.

Their first mission is to stay on the horse; their second is to make sure they know their orders and relay them correctly to their lieutenants. Then things should go smoothly. It will be a long march and a fast march as they will be short on time. They will be pulling cannons and wagons with supplies that will slow them down a lot, but they will still go as fast as possible.

Then General Benson Weaver gives the order to make camp and be prepared for anything, this is Yankee country. They are less than fifty miles from Washington, DC. The Confederacy is spread completely around the south side of Bull Run. Captain Marty Standish has by now learned how to stay on his horse very well and is ready for a fight. He has orders to take a platoon of fifty men and go to a Yankee camp, recon[1] it, then raid it and capture their officer with documents if possible.

Captain Marty wants to make sure he goes on this raid to show his men how to do a raid at night with no one ever knowing they were there. Captain Marty takes his platoon of men the afternoon before they go and tells them what their orders are. He then tells them, "We are not going to rush in on horseback shouting and screaming and shooting our guns. We are going in around 3:00 a.m. and quietly kill everyone in their sleep. I will show you how it is done quickly and quietly, while you move around fast. They are dead asleep. Most of them won't wake up for anything. Then we can leave with the officers and documents and never lose a man." Everyone liked the idea. At midnight the

---

[1] Recon is short for Reconnaissance

captain got his men gathered and they headed out for their mission. They got to the camp about 10 p.m. and the Captain and a dozen others went out to recon the camp. They waited and watched till they figured out where the officers' tents were, then they went back and told the others where the officers' tents were and who would attack which tents. He then told the men that they only need kill men in the surrounding tents around the officers. Kill all they needed till time to go, then they would leave and no one would know the difference till morning.

They would be on their way back to camp without a chase and no one hurt, with prisoners. They would all have plenty of dead to account for before the battle. Not only that but a story to tell back home.

When General Weaver got his report and found out the number of dead they left behind and no one knew they were there till morning, he was impressed. He put in for the captain to receive a medal right away. Then he sent a memo out to the other divisions of the operation. The men performed as a morale booster and to help the men see that the Yanks were not invincible.

The officers captured and the documents were a great help in finding the other Union soldier locations. What was most important was the three French officers that were brought in. The general noticed they were speaking freely in French to one another. So he dismissed himself and had Captain Standish come in and listen to their conversation. He advised him to say nothing, just stand at attention and take in everything the Frenchmen had to say till they were dismissed.

After the tent was cleared, The general called in his staff and Captain Standish. He asked Captain Standish what the French had to say and if anything was important. Captain Standish reported that that night a raid was going to hit General Lee's camp and try to capture General Lee and recover his documents. The general sent a rider right away with a written message to General Lee's camp, advising him of the attack. The message got there too late, but General Lee was safe and at another location at the time. They did get away with his attack plan, and he had to make a new plan. The next day the new plan was carried out and the first day of the battle of Bull Run was fought July 21, 1861.

There were around eighteen thousand men on both sides fighting in this battle. Most of them were untrained, undisciplined, and ragtag soldiers, fighting for their lives. The battle seemed to go back and forth as to who was winning in the morning, but as the day dragged on, the Confederacy started gaining more ground. By late afternoon, the Union soldiers were on the run for Washington, DC.

What made the difference? General Lee had put in charge of his forces Brig. General P.G.T. Beauregard, an experienced general in warfare and combat. This man held his ground.

President Abraham Lincoln had put in charge Brig. General Irvin McDowell, who had some experience in warfare. Yet, on the battlefield, he was not able to hold up to the pressure of the constant decision making, and at the end, made critical mistakes, causing his men to abandon their posts when under fire and head for Washington, D.C.

During the battle, Captain Marty Standish and his company of two hundred men were roaming the countryside looking for Union soldiers trying to outflank their men. It didn't take long before they had themselves a fight. They caught around three hundred Yanks crossing a young cornfield and going to a tree line along the forest. The Yanks were on foot, and Captain Standish and his men were on horseback.

The Yanks hadn't seen them, so the Captain ordered his men to go back to a spot that was not as thick with trees and undergrowth. Then they would ride their horses across to where the Yanks were crossing the field and wait. When they got close enough they would charge, screaming, yelling, firing their pistols, and using their swords.

These were exciting moments, waiting for the enemy to get into range so close you could see their eyes and their teeth when they gritted them. Then the Captain yelled as loud as he could, "Charge! Charge! Charge!" All two hundred men came out of the woods on horseback at point-blank range, shooting, yelling, and screaming, catching the enemy totally off guard. For about thirty minutes they fought, both sides, each man for their lives. When it was over the Union soldiers, what was left of them, had fled back across the cornfield as far as they could go. It was a special victory for the captain and his men.

The men told the captain that they felt the little bit of training in hand-to-hand combat he gave them made the difference in the battle. The captain said not to worry, and if they continued to apply themselves, he would teach them more as time went on. He did warn them, if he caught one man abusing his training, he would be transferred to another unit.

The captain's report to the general showed that he had less than an 8% death rate in his raid and severe casualties were low also. He gave the general the number of enemies that escaped, and less than 10% escaped. The general was impressed with him and his men's achievements again.

The general ordered the captain and his men to take a couple of days off and rest up for another assignment. They didn't get to rest up; the Battle of Bull Run was over that day with the Confederacy winning the battle. The day was Sunday, July 21, 1861, and people had come in their buggies and fancy wagons from Washington, D.C. to see the Battle of Bull Run, watching from far away on hilltops. When the battle was lost, they fled in a panic to get back to Washington to safety. Washington was only thirtyfive miles away from the battle.

Captain Standish sent his lieutenant with a platoon of fifty men toward the hill where the civilians were with orders to check for what might be of interest and look for Union prisoners. When the men returned, they had many Union prisoners, but best of all, they had New York Congressman Alfred Ely in custody. The general thought that was most impressive. The Congressman was questioned and put under arrest until the next day when a decision would be made as to where they would be sending him.

After a couple of days, word came from Confederate President Jefferson Davis that the Congressman was to be sent to Richmond, Virginia, under heavy guard. There he would be questioned by special agents that knew how to question him about the inside information they wanted to know. They knew he had first-hand information about the War that only skilled intelligence officers could get. They knew about the goings-on on the inside and how to use it against the Congressman, even to the point of bribery.

Captain Marty Standish has just received new orders. His company will leave the Corps sector and move to the state of North Carolina, temporarily, in Guilford County on the outskirts of the local towns in the area. There he will set up camp and patrol the countryside, searching for Union activities and protect the ammunition manufacturing plant in High Point. He will give daily reports to his commander by wire. If any activity is observed, notice must be sent right away. Then a decision of what size a regiment, a division, or larger is needed. Right away the captain had his men form a formation and told his men what their new orders were and what they needed to know. They were told to be ready to be on the move by sunup and after chow the next morning.

At sunrise, the formation was ready to go. Orderly, everyone rode down the road toward North Carolina to set up camp till they had new orders. They arrived in North Carolina at their destination about three weeks later, traveling slowly as time was no issue. They brought several cannons and wagons loaded with ammo and supplies.

There were orders that the captain did not reveal to his men. There was an ammunition manufacturing plant for the Confederacy in High Point, North Carolina that they were to protect, without giving the appearance of any discovery from the outside.

The ammunition plant was of vital importance, producing much arms, ammunition, and explosives for the Army. It was important that no one interfered with the production of arms, gun powder, or any other products they manufactured. Any interference was considered espionage, and if proven, one would face the death penalty. Captain Marty Standish served his time basically behind a desk. He did meet with the men for a workout every day and spent time going over hand-to-hand combat training. His men gave him their deepest respect and would do nothing to dishonor him or the company. The company was especially helpful to the local police force, bringing in lawbreakers.

Officers who knew of Captain Standish and his men's reputation as a fighting unit could not understand why they had city duty. Orders were sent to the captain for his company to head to Tennessee and join up with General Albert Johnston's command. They were expecting a large battle with the Union forces there in Tennessee. Johnston ordered Captain Standish to take his company to the river and search till he found a Union build-up of soldiers.

Captain Standish took his men and headed toward the river in search of Union forces. He had gone about a day's ride and come into contact with a patrol of around fifty Union soldiers on horseback. He had a scout go ahead of them as a point man when he came back to report the patrol. Captain Standish had all of his two hundred men line up on both sides of the trail. Orders were given to take prisoners if possible. Everyone waited patiently till the Union Cavalry was in position, then the order was given, "Charge! Charge! Charge!" The Union was hit so fast and hard they were completely surprised, and the ones who tried to fight back were thrown to the ground and subdued.

Captain Standish had his lieutenant take fifty men and take the prisoners back to camp to be questioned. He estimated where the location of their camp was based on the terrain of the area. His men split up into three platoons of fifty men each. He sent each platoon into a direction that he thought would pay off. Before long one of the platoons returned and reported that they had sighted Union forces in a tree grove about a mile north. Captain Standish told his men to get into ambush position in case he was spotted and troops followed him out. He would take his usual squad of scouts and get a closer look at their camp, checking for artillery placements.

It would be important for Confederate artillery to knock out the Union artillery at the beginning of a battle.

The captain sketched out a detailed picture of the camp and the artillery's location in detail. He went down to the camp as far as he could go, noting every detail. Suddenly one of the horses spooked, and a guard fired a shot, hitting the captain in his left shoulder. They rushed to their horses and about fifty Union soldiers pursued them. The men helped the captain onto his horse, and they rushed off to get help from the other men. When they came to the ambush area, the captain's men were ready. When the Union soldiers rode through, they were all cut down with no survivors. The captain was quickly examined by a doctor, treated temporarily, and then hurried away to their camp.

When the captain got back to camp, he was sent to the infirmary and operated on to take the rifle ball out of his left shoulder. Later, while he was in bed and resting, Colonel George Baker came in and praised him for the capture of the fifty prisoners. Then he asked why he didn't ride in and get the honor of bringing in the prisoners but instead sending his lieutenant. Then he risked his life, the life of a captain for information a lieutenant could have gotten. He then reached inside his coat and got the sketches of the Union camp and said the lieutenant could not have done this.

When the colonel saw the drawings, he could not believe his eyes. Everything was there that they needed to defeat the Union army at that location, even knocking out their artillery. The map was sent to General Albert Johnson who was waiting for orders to charge the Union camp. That camp was a regiment of over eight hundred men, well trained, along with a company of two hundred cavalry.

Orders were given to take the regiment of men and set for an attack at daybreak. After the artillery attack had been going on for fifteen minutes, then they were to attack during the artillery attack. The artillery attack will stop as they come into the fight.

The battle was a complete victory, the Union was driven back several miles in a great defeat. General Albert Johnson was shot in the left knee, hitting an artery. He was taken off his horse, put under a tree, and he bled to death in just a few minutes. General P.G.T. Beauregard was second in command and ordered a retreat at that time, which was a mistake for the South.

During the day, General Grant had gotten reinforcements and extra artillery. The next day at daybreak Southern forces were bombarded with artillery and heavy Union forces, driving the Confederacy back past the lines they gained the day before and far beyond. The South had lost a great battle known as the Battle Of Shiloh, fought on April, 6-7, 1862, with over thirteen thousand Union casualties and over ten thousand Confederate casualties. The map that Captain Standish drew saved many Southerners' lives and caused the deaths of many Union soldiers.

Captain Standish was building a chest full of medals, and he was admired by senior officers at their formal meetings. His company was the most decorated in the division and well known for its combat experience and skills. The Captain had been on many other combat missions in the past and had proven to be an exceptional combat officer.

The rumor that was going around was that the captain was going to get a promotion. It didn't take long before the news came in that the captain was promoted to Major Marty Standish. He was ordered to move to command a regiment of over eight hundred men in Virginia and to patrol toward Tennessee if called upon.

The Major had just one request, and that was that a squad of twelve men who he selected from his company go with him. The reason was they had been hand trained by him, and he needed them to help train a special company in his regiment. Permission was granted.

Major Standish and his squad arrive in Virginia and join the regiment he is assigned to, along with his special squad. The Major requests to have his squad assigned to a company to give them special combat training. His request is granted. He also asks that the company be under his command and that, too, is granted.

Now he can get to work using his guerrilla war tactics, working the area that is suspected to be a build-up for a battle. He has his company divided into four sections of fifty men with three of his trained scouts in each platoon. These three men would be teaching the other men guerrilla war tactics while they are in the bush. They will be working the area in southern Virginia, eastern Kentucky, and northeast Tennessee, making hit and run and ambush attacks on the Yankees, infiltrating camps, capturing officers, attacking soldiers in their sleep, and collecting documents. Major Standish's company of men was a real threat to the Union soldiers all over that area, for the short time they covered it. The Union was so threatened by his companies' activities, they had set a bounty on the heads of him and his men.

General Lee had ordered the division to report just west of Richmond about thirty-five miles and make camp till further orders and to have his men prepared for battle and ready to move in a moment's notice. Major Marty Standish and his men were always battle-ready at any notice. It took them the best part of a week to make the trip and get set in. Then when he had been brought up to date as to what the situation was and saw the maps, he was better able to advise his captains and lieutenants as to what to do from then on. Later, he met with his twelve scouts, advising them how to conduct their operations in the bush with the men.

He got orders from the colonel to start right away with his special company of men patrolling the area suspected of engagement. The four platoons split up and went in the separate directions suspected of enemy buildup. Each platoon, when they found a camp, would send about half their men at 3:00 a.m. into the camp stabbing, cutting throats, and moving swiftly throughout the tents, killing Yankee soldiers while others were capturing Union officers and collecting documents. Within less than ten minutes they were in and out. This was the same with all four platoons. Only one platoon had success in capturing a high-level officer. They spent the better part of the day before doing a recon of the area, making a drawing of the camp and especially of the artillery setup and their ammo dumps.

All four platoons got away without being noticed and never had to use their ambush that was set up. They made it back to camp, giving their reports to the major with their drawings. When the major had all the reports and the prisoners were taken care of, about 9:30 a.m., he made his report to the colonel and informed him of the prisoners. Right away he ordered intelligence to start interrogating the men. Then he and the major went over the report and the drawings, after the colonel clearly and cleverly understood the reports, he called a meeting of his staff. He informed them of the intelligence report that Major Marty Standish's company had gathered, and it was very impressive.

The Colonel had already taken the Majors report and sent it with his report to General Lee. The report was a major aid in helping General Lee arrange his attack of Gaines' Mill. The report showed areas that were not shown on the Confederate maps. This was interesting because he now knew where Union soldiers were that he never knew existed on the map before. He also knew the exact location of their artillery. This was information that money could not buy.

The general was waiting for General "Stonewall" Jackson's forces to come in, but they were running late. He could wait no longer, so he had to give the command for the men to move forward and attack. At first, the Union forces put up a solid fight as they were well dug in and fortified. Fighting continued until just before dusk then Jackson's reinforcements came in about midday. The Union forces were running out of ammunition and were exhausted and ready to give up. Then the Confederate rush came, driving them back across the Boatswain's Swamp and the James River until the next morning when they crossed the Chickahominy River in full retreat. As they crossed the Chickahominy River, they blew the bridge behind them. The Battle Of Gaines' Mill was fought on Friday, June 27, 1862.

General George McClellan finished other battles around Richmond and finally gave up trying to capture the Confederate capitol. At one point he got within a few miles of the Capitol in Richmond, yet, he was scared of General Lee, thinking he had far more men than he did, he was scared to attempt an attack. He later attacked him at other locations, winning most of those battles.

Major Marty Standish had orders for his regiment to stay and fight with the three divisions under Major General Richard Ewell. General Ewell was well known as a cavalry officer and loved to see the cavalry charge. He was usually under General Lee's Command when General Lee went into battle.

After the battle, they went back to camp and Major Standish had a letter from his brother Jay. Jay also had command of his own company as a captain, doing much of the same thing that Marty was doing. Marty gave him details of what he was doing with his men so he may pick up a few ideas if he needed any. Neither of the brothers had heard from the other men or from home. The way men were being killed, they were blessed to be alive. Turns out they are in many of the same battles because Jay spends a lot of time in Tennessee. Maybe now they can keep in contact.

Now General Lee wants to take the battle to the north. He wants to go to Maryland and get as near to Washington as he can to make a threat on Washington, D.C. The Maryland border is less than thirty-five miles from Washington, D.C. The General is sure he will be met by General McClellan and his Union forces somewhere in Maryland between him and Washington.

General Lee decides to send Major Marty Standish's special company towards the city of Sharpsburg, Maryland. That is the area where he expects General George McClellan and his forces to be located. He wants them to do their usual guerrilla war tactics, gathering information for him.

On September 11, the major reported that he and his scouts, on their recon patrols, had observed massive columns of Union soldiers on the move. General Lee had plans to hit Washington but decided to withdraw to the South and meet General McClellan at Sharpsburg, Virginia, where he had set in. Major Standish had given him a good description of the layout of his troops and his artillery positions. Sharpsburg is around sixty miles from Washington.

General Lee was concerned about his supply lines coming up from the south, and he needed the railroad junction at Harper's Ferry, along with the river supply line. Harper's Ferry blocked that supply line and had to be destroyed. He split his forces and had General "Stonewall" Jackson take his troops along with General Hill's forces to take Harper's Ferry.

General Jackson arrived on the twelfth and started the attack, but the Yankees held strong. The fighting continued as General Hill's men joined the fight, adding more artillery. On the morning of the fifteenth General "Stonewall" Jackson set fifty artillery guns around General Miles' forces and began firing at daylight. Then he ordered his men to a full charge against the Union forces. At that time General Miles met with his officers, and they decided to raise the white flag and surrender. Twelve thousand Union prisoners were taken, and General Hill was to stay behind with his men to clear up the details of the surrender. General Miles was wounded by an artillery shell and died the next day. The Battle of Harper's Ferry ran from September 12 to 15, 1862.

General "Stonewall" Jackson took his men and went straight toward Sharpsburg, Maryland. He had his men on a forced march all night till they got to Sharpsburg the next day in the afternoon. Then joining up with Lee's forces, he greatly increased the size of General Lee's army.

General McClellan had estimated General Lee's forces at one hundred twenty thousand men much larger than what General Lee's forces were at that time. He sent out reconnaissance missions to get more information, but the information was not that good as General Jackson arrived the next afternoon.

General Lee had his forces in a parcel of a halfcircle around Antietam, facing General McClellan's forces. He had Major Standish and his men infiltrate the Union lines and capture some documents. This was helpful as to their artillery placements. It was important to knock out the artillery as soon as possible. The Union artillery usually had a longer range than most of the Confederate's, making it out of their range. With this information, they could move their artillery closer to their position.

The left wing of Lee's forces was commanded by General "Stonewall" Jackson, and the right was commanded by General Longstreet. General A.P. Hill's division had remained at Harper's Ferry, but on the morning of the 17th, he got orders to march as quickly as possible to Antietam. That march would be around seventeen miles, but it would take some time to get organized and prisoners put away.

General McClellan had a problem in that he was too cautious, always expecting the unexpected that was never there. He estimated General Lee's forces to be twice as large as they were. He held back divisions of men in reserve that could have been used in battle and that would have defeated the South with ease. He avoided a battle because he feared Lee had the advantage when he didn't. He was slow about making his decisions an indecisive man. General Lee was just the opposite!

The South didn't have the power, productivity of industry, money, men, guns, and so on. Yet, they somehow made what they had work for them. General Lee seemed to be the best they had, and at the time, he was a long way from being perfect.

The battle began at daylight on the Confederate's left. Hooker's corps came charging over the cornfield, losing one-fourth of his men in the attack. Hooker himself was shot in the foot and carried off the field. Command was then given to Brigadier General Meade. General Jackson's divisions had even more causalities as the day went on, losing his generals and colonels. General John B. Hood and D.H. Hill arrived, helping Jackson to hold its ground.

Major General Joseph Mansfield's XII Corps attacked from the left and caused a lot of damage to the southerners. Mansfield was killed during the battle and Brig. General Alpheus Williams led the Yankees, and General Hood and General Hill were driven back to a holding point. The fight was then at a standstill till the end with both sides losing several thousands of men.

On the southern end of the Union lines, General Burnside

got his orders late. When he acted General Lee had shifted most of his troops from the southern side to help General Jackson in the north. Finally, Burnside made his move with some of the men left behind. They were joined by around five hundred Georgian sharpshooters covering the bridge and farther down the creek.

General Burnside spent several hours trying to force his way across the creek, but it was too costly. Finally, the Southern boys had almost run out of ammunition, and after a Union charge with bayonets, they retreated.

Burnside now crossed the Antietam with his division of men and attacked the entrance, the Confederate men of General Lee did the best they could at the time. Burnside thought he had defeated Lee's army that day when he heard for the first time the "Rebel Yell." It was coming from General A.P. Hill's division from Harper's Ferry. They had arrived in the nick of time. They were newly supplied with food and supplies from Harper's Ferry when the supply wagons arrived.

The Battle of Antietam was to be the bloodiest day in US history and lasted less than twelve hours. General McClellan was ordered to continue the engagement but refused. General Lee and his troops crossed the Potomac without any more engagements with the enemy. General McClellan expected General Lee to attack Washington and returned to Washington to set up a defense. President Lincoln then gave him orders to pursue Robert E. Lee's army across the Potomac to Virginia. He was then to destroy his army.

General McClellan took his army and head for the Potomac; it took him nine days to cross the Potomac River. President Lincoln was so disappointed at his putting things off again, that he sent orders relieving the General of his command and giving it to General Burnside.

General Burnside made his rounds, going through Virginia and parts of Kentucky and chasing rumors about General Lee while General Lee was building up and strengthening his army. Every day he was adding more men and supplies and getting stronger for an attack up north.

It is the month of November now and General Robert E. Lee is headed toward the north to Fredericksburg, Virginia. He is ready for a big battle with General Burnside.

His army is packed and ready. His supply line is on the move, and he is headed toward a place called Fredericksburg, Virginia. He expects to arrive around the first of December. There he expects to meet up with General Burnside and have another battle just fifty-eight miles from Washington, D.C.

General Burnside is planning to cross the Rappahannock River and then continue for the next 184 miles to Roanoke, Virginia, the Confederate Capitol. Yet, he has a problem when he reaches the River Rappahannock.

There are no pontoon bridges there to get his one hundred thousand men across the river. They have to wait almost a week before they arrive. By that time General Lee has arrived and set up positions across the Rappahannock River. When the men start setting the pontoon bridge in place, the sharpshooters begin picking off the workers.

It takes quite a while, but the job is finally finished. Then General Burnside gives the order to charge. Even then they had a problem getting their men across the river, it took the rest of the day and night and didn't finish till the next day. The battle started December 11, 1862, a Thursday, and there was deadly fighting going on all day. General Burnside had General Franklin take just one of his six divisions under his command and make an attack on General "Stonewall" Jackson's troops. The attack failed, and General Jackson made a successful counter-attack, which drove the Union forces back with heavy casualties.

Lieutenant General James Longstreet's corps held Marye's Heights. General Burnside ordered Maj. General Darius Couch's corps to attack the Confederate forces with a bayonet charge. There was a field over six hundred yards long with General Longstreet's Rebel soldiers behind a stone wall, ready to fire. It was a killing field; a man never got as close as fifty feet to the wall. That day General Burnside sent fourteen attacks against that wall. On December 14, the General considered sending more attacks against the wall, but his officers talked him out of it. The night before was a night of freezing temperatures and the General ask for a cease-fire to collect their dead and wounded. Most of the wounded froze to death overnight. On Monday, December 15, 1862, under a truce, the Yankees collected their wounded and dead, and under the cover of darkness and rain, they escaped to the north. General Robert E. Lee had a great victory for the South at Fredericksburg, Virginia. It built greatly needed morale for the Confederacy. The general and his men remained in Fredericksburg for some time to rest and reorganize. The casualties for the North were 12,653; the casualties for the South were 4,201. The Battle Of Fredericksburg started on Thursday, December 11, 1862, and ended on Monday, December 15, 1862.

THE END OF THE WAR

CHAPTER TEN
Marty Standisch Fighting till the End

The Battle of Fredericksburg is over, and now the war has moved into the new year, 1863. Everyone awaits what this year will bring. Will it bring more or less death? Only time will tell!

Major General Joseph Hooker has taken charge of the Union Army of the Potomac, by order from President Abraham

Lincoln. The Eastern theater for January has been quiet. Most of the battles were in the states of Texas, Missouri, Arkansas, and Idaho. They were not large engagements, except for one in Arkansas on January 9-11, 1863. The war in January was mild compared to the past.

At the end of February, there was a military build-up of Union troops in Tennessee. The entire month of February was a month of little to no major activity, just a few ambushes and hit and run attacks. Major Standish and his men were busy searching out the enemy and doing recon patrols on their camps. When he reported the build-ups in Tennessee, his commanding officer gave him orders to have his regiment report to the small town of Murfreesboro, Tennessee. That is almost in the center of Tennessee, sitting almost halfway between Nashville and Chattanooga, Tennessee.

There his men could make patrols in all directions around the center of Tennessee and should be able to spot a large army build-up that might be headed toward a major Tennessee city or Confederate outpost.

Dover
February 3, 1863

On February 3, 1863, at Dover, Tennessee, there was a battle in which the Confederates tried to conquer the Union forces.

The Yankees had taken control of the Cumberland River and controlled shipping going in and out of the river. It was important that they be moved out. Major General Joseph Wheeler took two brigades, that is around 8,000 men, and went to Dover, Tennessee, to drive them out. When the battle started General Wheeler used his artillery and charged the Union brigade, but they were driven back each time. He finally said they were too well secured, and he gave up the fight, retreating with a loss of 670 men to 126 Union men. He had 8,000 men to their 4,000. There were several other battles in Tennessee during February but not of major size. Major Standish and his company of special forces were busy making their rounds through Tennessee. One of his platoons found a cave near a company of Yankees camped out, and they continuously harassed them for a month, cutting the Union's size in half before their hideout was discovered and the Union got reinforcements. Then they had to pull out and find another location.

Fighting in March was light everywhere, but April was different. There were a lot of battles scattered over the country from the east to the west and very heavy around Arkansas and Mississippi.

Captain Jay Standish and his company of cavalrymen were ordered to go to Chancellorsville and join General Robert E. Lee's forces. They arrived on April 30 and set up camp while the Captain went to receive more orders. He was ordered to recon the outside areas within twenty-five miles for possible Union campsites and take notes of all information possible: artillery count, cavalry, foot soldiers, and supply lines. Then he was to report back as soon as possible to General Lee's camp with the information.

When Captain Jay Standish submitted the information that he had gathered, General Lee knew that General Joseph Hooker was trying to trap his forces into a major battle at Chancellorsville. So he started setting his men into a defensive position, preparing for an attack.

General Hooker had troops attack General Lee's supply line several times outside Fredericksburg, Virginia but could not stop them.

Chancellorsville
April 30-May 6, 1863

On April 30 General Hooker tried to attack General Lee from his front and rear at the same time. He had no success, and on May the first General Hooker advanced toward General Lee, but General Lee split his army. General Lee left a small force at Fredericksburg to attack Major General John Sedgwick's forces.

He then marched on toward Chancellorsville. Hooker withdrew to Chancellorsville, digging in with his forces and his artillery ahead of General Lee and his army. General Hooker had far superior forces, twice as many as General Lee.

On May the second, General Lee again split his army, sending General "Stonewall" Jackson on a flank march toward the Union XI Corps. When General Jackson got his men set in, he wanted to make a recon of the area. The Yankees were just beyond their lines; it was a full moon, and he knew their approximate location. He just needed to see where to make the main attack from. After he got his information he and his men headed back. They were mistaken for Yankee soldiers and fired at in the dark. Three rifle balls hit General "Stonewall" Jackson in the left arm and his arm had to be amputated. The operation caused problems, and the general caught pneumonia and died eight days later. Major General J.E.B. Stewart took command of the Corps Command.

May third was a day of many battles in Chancellorsville, with many losses on both sides. Although the Union had twice the number of men, they did not have the advantages. Lee's artillery positions were on the higher ground and better located than Hooker's most of the time. That made a big difference in the way the battles went most of the time.

At 9:15 a.m., General Hooker was leaning against a wooden pillar when a cannonball hit it. He was unconscious for over an hour, and when he did come to he was distorted and distracted, mentally disturbed, and confused. He no doubt received a concussion but was not relieved of his command. The telegraph lines were out, and there were lost communications with much of his army throughout the battle. The General was making unwise decisions, like ordering one regiment off a hill to another location. The officer was quoted as saying, "God, if we can't hold them on top of the hill, how will we at the bottom?"

On May 4, General Hooker held his position at his location without trying to make any advances. General Lee again split his forces, sending them to attack General Sedgwick's forces. They attacked Sedgwick's forces and drove them back toward the Rappahannock River. When Hooker realized that Sedgwick had retreated across the Rappahannock River, he immediately met with his commanding officers and asked for a decision to retreat or to fight. They decided to retreat as soon as possible.

General Hooker and all his men retreated on the nights of May 5 and 6 to the river at the shallow river crossing called the U.S. Ford and crossed without any attacks. Sedgwick's Army retreated across the Rappahannock's Bank's Ford during the pre-dawn hours of May 5, 1863.

The Battle of Chancellorsville started on April 30, 1863, continuing until May 6, 1863, and was a Confederate victory. Forces engaged in the battle were numbered at 154,734. Union forces numbered 97,382, and Confederate forces numbered 57,352. The total number of estimated casualties was 30,764. The Union forces' casualties numbered 17,304, and the Confederate's were 13,460.

Siege Of Vicksburg
May 18-July 4, 1863

The next major battle fought in the Civil War was not considered a battle but a siege, "The Siege of Vicksburg" was fought not between General Lee and General Hooker but between Major General Ulysses S. Grant of the Union and Lieutenant General John C. Pemberton of the Confederacy. These battles were not fought in the east but in Mississippi and Louisiana.

Grant started his fight by going around toward Louisiana and working his way back toward and then capturing the Mississippi Capitol. He then had General Sherman destroy anything that was connected to the South's military: railroad, telegraph, post office, anything. They destroyed the city and towns around for miles. Then they headed for Vicksburg to join General Grant to take Vicksburg.

At Champion Hill, Lt. General John C. Pemberton put up a

battle against Grant's forces, but they could not hold. Grant's men tried to flank the Rebels' side leading to Vicksburg and block their escape. The Rebels held out and were able to escape to Vicksburg. All night they spent digging in for the fight of their lives; they knew what was coming. It didn't come right away, so they still had time to make more reinforcements. On the nineteenth of May, General Sherman and his XV Corps attacked at a log stockade wall across the Graveyard Road connecting two gun positions that were manned by rifle pits. Sherman's men moved forward down the road about 2 p.m. and were slowed down by ravines and combat obstacles mounted in their way. Sherman gave the order to attack. Edward C. Washington, the grandnephew of George Washington, commanding a regiment's First Battalion was killed in the attack. After the bloody attack, Sherman's men pulled back.

Grant decided to make a more thorough reconnaissance of the defense before he would order another attack and where he would concentrate his fire. On the morning of May 22, the Union artillery hit the Southern forces for four hours without letting up. At 10 a.m. the artillery stopped, and the Union forces started their infantry attack against a three-mile front.

Sherman started his attack down Graveyard Road. Later, his men faced a ditch that was ten feet deep and had walls twenty feet high with rifle and artillery fire. At the breach of the railroad, they were faced with bloody hand-to-hand combat. The Union finally won the attack but took only a handful of prisoners, while that was their only victory for the day.

Grant then decided to siege Vicksburg. Vicksburg was then under constant bombardment from Grant's army artillery or from the Navy gunboats till its surrender.

By early June, Grant had set up thirteen points along his lines where he ordered tunnels to be dug under the Confederate positions. Then they were to place as much as 2,200 pounds of black powder in the tunnels, and on June 25 detonate it, causing a large explosion. It blew a twelve-foot deep crater, after which there was a 20-hour hand-to-hand combat battle. The Union forces could not advance and had to retreat.

By July the situation had gotten to the point that the Confederacy was in a serious condition. They were sick and wounded with no food or water and no ammo that amounted to much. On July 3, Grant and Pemberton meet to discuss surrender. Grant wanted an unconditional surrender, but Pemberton refused and went back to Vicksburg. General Grant wanted to end the siege and move on to take over the Mississippi River and split the Confederacy. So that night General Grant offered to parole the Confederate defenders of Vicksburg. The Confederates lowered their flag and marched out, stacking their rifles and thus ending the forty-seven-day siege of Vicksburg.

With General Pemberton's army defeated and destroyed, the Union army now marched on to Port Hudson, and five days later the Confederacy was split in half with the Union navy patrolling the Mississippi.

Battle of Vicksburg, Virginia

The Total Number of Forces Involved:
110,000
Union 77,000   Confederate 33,000

Total Casualties
37,273

Killed
Union 806   Confederate 805

Wounded
Union 3,940   Confederate 1,938

Missing/Captured
Union 164   Confederate 29,620

Totals
Union 4,910   Confederate 32,363

General Grant split the Confederacy by taking control of the Mississippi River and winning the Battle of Vicksburg, which made him a hero. He got President Abraham Lincoln's attention as an effective General in the war against the Southern states. General Grant was a smart and decisive man. When he made his decision, it was usually one that was well thought out. He used recon information as much as possible when making his plan for an attack. General Grant's battles would then be to clean up the area of the Confederates.

Gettysburg
July 1-3, 1863

The next major battle was to be fought at Gettysburg, Virginia, from July 1 till July 3. Yet there was much more fighting. For days before and days after the battle, there were battles between the North and South.

General Stewart had orders to take three brigades of cavalry and search for the Army of the Potomac. When he had reached his location, the army had moved and was no longer there. He was to safely hold the mountain passes; Stewart was to move east of the South Mountain and then cross the Potomac River. He was then to gather supplies and create chaos every chance he got as he tried to link up with Lt. General Richard S. Ewell's Second Corps.

Stewart rode out on June 25 and fell behind schedule. He found Major General Winfield S. Hancock's entire Federal II Corps spread out in the valley below. After some skirmishing and ambushes, Stewart broke off and withdrew. He then passed around the Union forces and battled with the Union cavalry near Fairfax Court House. While at the courthouse, they plundered the Federal supply depot and restocked with supplies. Then his troops crossed the Potomac River at Rowser's Ford and headed north. They captured and destroyed 150 wagons near Rockville, Maryland, on June 28 and fought with a Delaware cavalry at Westminster, Maryland on June 29, 1863.

The next day General Stewart was in a battle with Kilpatrick's Third Division all day at Hanover, PA. Cavalry on both sides were fighting in the streets of Hanover and killing with vicious fighting. A newly promoted Brig. General George A. Custer, commanding the Michigan horse soldiers joined the fighting. General Stewart had to break off and withdraw his soldiers, heading toward York, PA. General Stewart was almost captured. He was cornered on a street with no way out except to ride his horse as fast as he could to the end of the street and jump a large ditch.

General Stewart arrived near York and learned that the Confederate infantry had pulled out the day before.

So he marched to the nearby city of Carlisle at about 6:00 a.m.

What he did find was the Union infantry instead, so he set up his artillery for an attack. This was an important Federal military base and was destroyed while the city was set ablaze and burned.

One of General Stewart's staff reported that General Lee had the Confederate army collected at Gettysburg and were attacking. He then gathered his men and force-marched toward Gettysburg late at night. He would join General Lee and his forces midafternoon on July 2 in Gettysburg. This would be the bloodiest fight he and his men would encounter for some time during the war.

During the battle of Gettysburg, many battles were going on at the same time around the city. Shortly after 7:00 a.m. on July 1, Major General Heth's division approached Lt. General Hill's Third Corps, marching east. There was much fighting as General Heth's skirmishers faced stout resistance from the troops of Colonel W. Gamble's brigade. The next day Buford's two brigades were taken off the fighting line and sent to Maryland to guard the supply lines.

On July 1, the Confederate Forces were delayed because of the breech-loading carbine rifles that the Union army had. They were firing from behind fences, rocks, and trees, yet the Rebels had pushed the Yankee cavalrymen back to McPherson Ridge.

The Union Iron Brigade was commanded by Solomon Meredith, who was proving to be a successful officer after defeating General Archer in battle and taking several hundred men captive including General Archer himself. General Reynolds was shot and killed early in the fighting while directing troops and artillery positions.

Major General Abner Doubleday took over command, and fighting lasted until around 12:30 p.m. It started up again at 2:30 p.m.

General Pettigrew's North Carolina Brigade of 839 men came on the scene, flanked the 19th Indiana, and drove the Iron Brigade back with heavy losses. On July the second, General Lee's battle plan was for an assault on General Meade's positions. General Lee gave General Ewell orders to attack Culp's Hill and Cemetery Hill when he heard gunfire from Longstreet's attack.

This would prevent General Meade from shifting his troops to his left for support.

Longstreet moved past Meade and attacked his left flank, capturing the supply trains and blocking Meade's escape route. General Lee gave the order to attack at 11:00 a.m., but General Longstreet's First Corps did not get into position until 1:00 p.m. Generals Hood and McLaws had a long march and did not make an attack until after 4:00 and 5:00 p.m.

On July 2, General Gregg's division arrived from Hanover. His men attacked the Confederate infantry at Brinkerhoff's Ridge, which stopped the Confederates from joining the fighting on Culp's Hill.

General Kilpatrick's Third Division had another encounter with General Hampton's Cavalry Brigade. A violent attack broke out with a mounted charge lead by General Custer himself. Suddenly Custer's horse was shot out from under him and he went crashing to the ground. His orderly quickly grabbed the General, taking him to safety and from being captured. As darkness fell the fighting came to a halt.

The next morning, July 3, General Gregg recognized the importance of the intersection of the Hanover and Low Dutch Road. The Low Dutch Road was a direct route to the Union army. General Gregg had his men with Union infantry on Wolf's Hill join forces. Heavy fighting broke out in the fields around the farm of John Rummell. Stewart's men took heavy casualties in the engagement. General Custer took the lead in the charge and the Southerners fell back, reorganized, and then Stewart ordered a counter charge.

The Union artillery was blasting away at them as they charged; however, they never slowed down but kept charging. The artillery was doing its damage, yet they never looked back. It was a full charge to the battle line. The blades of sabers were flying in the air as the horsemen flashed by. General Custer was at the lead of the First Michigan Cavalry yelling "come on you Wolverines!" That charge split the Confederate line in two. The confused Confederates broke off and fell back, with heavy losses on both sides. General Stewart gave up his quest to take the intersection at Hanover and Low Dutch Roads. The fight for East Cavalry Field was over.

The main battlefield was only six or seven miles away from where they had been fighting. Brig. General Wesley Merritt's Regulars made a mounted charge around Lee's right flank. They had no support and had to fall back; their attack was a failure. Fighting back and forth continued till dark, and they pulled back.

General Merritt was told of a Confederate wagon train about ten miles west, so he decided to send a regiment to destroy the wagon train and report back. When they arrived, they found a brigade of Confederate soldiers defending the wagon train. After a violent fight with the Rebels, the regulars retreated with heavy losses, and their Commander, Major Samuel H. Starr, was left with severe wounds. Again, an example of another regiment operating behind enemy lines without any support.

Around 1:00 p.m., close to 170 Confederate artillery guns began a bombardment that lasted till around 3:00 p.m. Then 12,500 Confederate soldiers charged three-quarters of a mile toward Cemetery Ridge in what is known as "Pickett's Charge." They were meet with artillery from the North, which they thought was destroyed. After the charge, only about half of the men made it back to their own lines.

General Custer was said to be a twenty-threeyear- old General and a war hero of the Civil War.

The Battle of Gettysburg ended on the evening of July 3 at dark. The fighting on the way out was bad in many places. It took till July fourth to get organized enough to pull out in the evening. They were headed toward the Potomac River Crossing at the Ford. Heavy rains fell for several days, and the Potomac raised to flood stage. The pontoon bridge across the river at Falling Waters was not under protection by General Lee's army and was destroyed by the Union cavalry.

Brig. General John D. Imboden's cavalry was escorting a wagon train that that was filled with wounded men headed home in the rain. They were trying to get to the river crossing and were constantly being attacked by Union cavalry. On July 6 General Stewart's men defeated General Kilpatrick's division at Hagerstown. On July 8 Stewart attacked Buford's men at Boonsboro in a full day of vicious fighting. General Stewart finished the day with a fight in his favor.

On July 12 General Lee's engineers built a strong defensive wall along the north bank of the Potomac River. After two days of light fighting, General Meade decided he would attack with his entire army. On the night of the thirteenth, the river had dropped so low that Lee's engineers could build a pontoon bridge at Falling Waters. All of Lee's army had moved out by morning except for a division of Hill's Corps, and they had to fight their way across then cut the ropes holding the bridge which went down the river and was destroyed.

Battle of Gettysburg

Commanders

Union		Confederate
General George G. Meade		General Robert E. Lee

Total Forces 165,620

Union		Confederate
93,921		71,699

Casualties
51,112

Union		Confederate
23,049		28,063

Killed

Union		
3,155		3,903

Wounded

Union		Confederate
14,529		18,735

Missing/Captured

Union		Confederate
5,365		5,425

Many more battles were fought but no more major battles of any size until the Battle of the Wilderness. The Battle of Cold Harbor was also a one-sided battle that the Union lost badly.

Major Marty Standish was at the Battle of Gettysburg, fighting with General Stewart. So was his brother Captain Jay Standish, fighting with General A. P. Hill's cavalry. Major Marty Standish had been in many battles and conflicts with the Yankees, and the same for his brother. Both men were well decorated for their combat abilities and achievements. They both had taught their men how to fight and survive well. Now they would spend time together and celebrate because the next day they would go their separate ways again.

Over the next year, many battles are fought in the east, the south, and in the western parts of the United States. The next major battle was on the horizon. It started May 5, 1864, and it was the first battle between Lt. General Ulysses S. Grant and General Robert E. Lee. The battle was called the Battle of the Wilderness. There were many losses on both sides, but the Union suffered the most losses by far. The Confederacy came out victorious; however the Yankees will say that they think they came out the winner.

The Battle of the Wilderness
May 5-7, 1864

The cause of the wilderness thickness started when earlier settlers came and settled. They found iron ore, and to melt the ore, they had to heat the blast furnaces so hot that they would melt the ore and separate it from the waste. So they had to use a lot of wood, especially hardwood. They began cutting trees everywhere in that area, till all the trees were gone. This left a rough terrain that was too rough to be settled, with washed-out places, ravines, gullies, and rocks. What grew back years later, was a thick wilderness of big high underbrush, small to medium size trees, and shrubs with some of the area left in a swamp-like condition, being close to the river.

Yes, it was ten months later that the Battle of the Wilderness started on Thursday, May 5 and lasted until May 7, 1864. General Robert E. Lee correctly predicted that General Grant would cross to the east of the Confederate fortifications on the Rapid River, using the Germanna and Ely Fords. This was to avoid contact with the Confederacy, giving General Lee notice of his whereabouts. General Lee guessed that General Grant would take that route, and later the reconnaissance patrols he had sent to scout out where the Yankees were proved him correct. General Lee knew then that they would meet somewhere close to Spotsylvania Court House by way of Chancellorsville. He then decided to prepare for battle and contacted General Ewell's Second Corps to meet him there. By May 4, his plan was being put into position.

He knew the wilderness battle would be his best fight because he was outnumbered two to one. The North had approximately 120,000 fighting men while the South had approximately 65,000. Both armies have fought much, and their men have come down in numbers quite a bit. By fighting in the wilderness, his men had the advantage.

They were better at close combat and had time to learn the terrain. General Grant's artillery will not be very effective in the wilderness, if at all.

On May 5, General Warren's V Corps was advancing over farmland toward Plank Road when General Ewell's Corps appeared, General Meade halted his army and instructed General Warren to attack, thinking it was a small isolated group of Rebels. General Warren approached the eastern side with a division on his right and a division on his left. He hesitated to attack because the Confederate positions went further on his right. General Warren asked for General Meade to have the VI Corps come in and fill in his right. General Meade was angry and ordered General Warren to attack.

General Warren was right about the extra Confederates at his right flank. When he attacked, General Ayres's brigade had to take cover in a gully. General Bartlett forced his attack against General John M. Jones, and General Jones was killed in the fighting. General Bartlett's horse was shot and killed out from under him, and he barely escaped being captured.

The famous Iron Brigade under Brig. General Lysander Cutler charged through the woods and attacked a brigade of Alabamians fighting under Brig. Cullen A. Battle. They pushed the Rebels back for a while till they counter-attacked with Brig. General John B. Gordon charging through the woods. The Iron Brigade was in full retreat, the Rebels yelling just behind them until they were all well out of the woods.

Near the Higgerson farm, Colonel Roy Stone and Brig. General James C. Rice attacked the brigades of Brig. General George P. Dole's Georgians and Brig. General Junius Daniel's North Carolinians. Stone and Rice, with their brigades, made two attacks and failed at both under heavy fire. General Crawford ordered his men to pull back, while General Warren tried to get artillery into Saunders Field to cover his attack. The problem was that it was captured by the Confederacy. During the hand-to-hand combat, the field caught fire, and the wounded from both sides were burned to death.

Fighting again started at the edge of Saunders Field around 3 p.m. General Sedgwick attacked General Ewell's line at the wood line. There were attacks and counter-attacks that lasted for about an hour, and then it stopped.

A mile to the rear, near the Orange Plank Road, General Lee, Jeb Stewart, and General Hill were meeting when a party of Union soldiers came into the clearing. The three Generals ran for safety, while the group of Union soldiers charged for cover in the woods. That day they could have changed the war if they had charged the enemy instead of the woods. Night fell on Thursday, May 5, the first day of the Battle of the Wilderness. Fighting in most places continued until dark.

Friday, May 6, 1864, was the second day of the Battle of the Wilderness. General Grant was concerned about the way things went the day before. Yet, he felt that General Hill's Confederate corps was worn out from fighting, low on ammo, and without much of a fight left in them. So he made this his target for the coming battle. At the same time, the V Corps and the VI Corps were to continue their attacks on General Ewell's positions, trying to stop him from coming to the aid of General Hill.

General Lee had decided to let General Hill rest while General Longstreet's corps, only ten miles away, march overnight to reinforce him in the morning. General Longstreet decided he had time to let his men stop and rest, so they stopped and rested. When they started again it was dark, and after traveling a while they got lost. It took a while, but their scouts got them back in the right direction, but they were not at their location at sunrise.

General Hancock's II Corps hit General Hill at 5 a.m. with an all-out attack, trying to overrun Hill's position. General Ewell's men on the turnpike attacked at 4:45 a.m. but were pinned down by General Sedgwick's and General Warren's corps. They were in a position where they could not be relieved. General Longstreet counter- attacked with the divisions of General Charles W. Field and General Joseph B. Kershaw.

The Union troops were still disorganized from the attack earlier that morning and weren't ready for another attack, so they had to fall back, retreating from the Widow Tapp Farm. A group of Texans led the fighting against the Yankees, a group of eight hundred men of which only about two hundred fifty survived. General Longstreet's chief engineer reported that he had found an unfinished railroad trackbed south of Plank Road, and it went to the Union's left flank.

Brig. General William Mahone struck the left flank with an attack, and it was a complete surprise, taking over the whole left flank. General Longstreet continued his attack driving General Hancock's men back to the Brock Road. There at that battle, General James S. Wadsworth was killed.

General Longstreet was riding with several of his officers along Plank Road when he came upon some of General Mahone's men. They believed the riders were Union cavalry and began firing. General Longstreet was wounded in the neck, and Brig. General Micah Jenkins was killed. General Charles Field took temporary command, and the next day General Lee assigned Maj. General Richard H. Anderson as temporary command of the First Corps. General Longstreet did not return to the Northern Virginia Army until October 13, 1864.

On May the seventh there were a few battles but nothing major. General Grant had noticed that the Confederates were well fortified and dug in. He decided to take his army and go toward Spotsylvania Court House at the crossroads and make a stand.

With General Lee's great network of spies, reconnaissance

patrols, and invasions of the tents of officers, he was way ahead of General Grant! General Lee had his reinforcements and the troops he could spare already on the move toward Spotsylvania while the others prepared to move. This before General Grant had given the order to break camp. When General Grant reached Spotsylvania, General Lee was there and well fortified..

Battle of the Wilderness

Commanders

Union	Confederate
Ulysses S. Grant	Robert E. Lee
George G. Meade	

Strength

Union	Confederate
101,895	61,025

Casualties

Union	Confederate
17,666	11,033

Killed

Union	Confederate
2,246	1,477

Wounded

Union	Confederate
12,037	7,866

Missing/Captured

Union	Confederate
3,383	1,690

This was the end of the Battle of the Wilderness. It lasted from Thursday, May 5, 1864, until May 7, 1864. It was a battle that General Lee was said to have won. It has always been said that the Union usually had twice as many men and guns as the Confederacy. Yet, they had trouble winning all the battles. The difference was the Southerners were mostly outdoorsmen with better shooting skills and leadership that knew how to deal with men.

Spotsylvania Court House
May 9-21, 1864

Grant was now headed toward Richmond and not Washington, D.C., like the generals before him to rest and resupply. General Grant knew that General Lee had to rest and resupply also. So he continued to press toward the south to Richmond. General Lee knew he had to go through Spotsylvania, from the reconnaissance reports that his men had stolen from General Grant's officers' tents.

General Anderson's infantry was on a forced march headed south toward Spotsylvania, to set up their position. About 8:00 a.m. on May 8 they made a stand on the Spindle Field, about a mile from the courthouse. They threw down fence rails and stacked them to fight behind. They held long enough for General Anderson's Corps to arrive on the field.

The Union infantry advanced across Spindle Field and the Confederate cavalrymen shouted for their infantry to run to their rail piles. By reaching the rail piles, they were able to fight the Yankees back and stop their drive.

Other Confederate units arrived in time to extend their line of attack. Several other Union attacks came but were unsuccessful. Although they were close to breaking through, the Confederate line held.

General Sheridan had been reporting to General Meade that he could destroy General Jeb Stewart's cavalry if he was turned loose on him. Over and over he kept saying this and General Meade was reporting it to General Grant. General Grant knew he needed Sheridan's cavalry too much for reconnaissance patrols, keeping him informed of enemy movements.

General Grant finally gave in to General Sheridan's request, making what he knew was a great mistake. It did prove to be a mistake when one looked at the overall cost to the Army of the Potomac. The cavalry provided intelligence reports of enemy movement for many battles. Without those reports, the Union lost many lives and positions.

General Sheridan did defeat General Stewart at Yellow Tavern, and General Stewart was mortally wounded. General Grant was left in a position for the next several days not knowing exactly what the Confederate positions or movements were.

The night of May 8 found General Grant's, forces in a state of confusion and disorganized. In the meantime, the Confederacy was taking up defensive positions along hills and ridges with open fields at their front, constructing a defensive barrier with stones, fences, trees, and anything else that would stop a rifle ball.

On May 9, 1864, Confederate officers noticed that they had formed a U-shape with their defense. The men called it the "Mule Shoe" because of its shape. General Lee was afraid it was weak to attack on three sides, but other officers convinced him that it was a strong defense and could be defended with artillery. They felt it would hold for days if needed. General Lee did order a well dug in line, across the base of the "Mule Shoe."

Many attempts were made at the Confederates, but they were always driven back. The Union losses were mounting up with each attack. There was a Colonel Emory Upton who thought that attacking a well-constructed defensive over and over with no results had to be changed. They had been moving up, stopping, firing, and loading, moving up, stopping, firing, and loading. Then they would retreat. What if they ran as far as they could to get a good aim, stop, fire, and then do a bayonet charge.

On the evening of May 8, General Ulysses S. Grant was watching the battle of the "Mule Shoe" and got a surprise that he needed. Colonel Emory Upton decided to put his idea to action to see if it would work. It did work, and his men went all the way to the Confederate defenses and were crossing over. They didn't have enough reinforcements, though, and had to pull back. General Grant called him in and asked him about his idea, then he promoted him to Brigadier General Upton. General Grant decided he was going to use that maneuver on a large scale with support troops behind the assault line.

May 11 turned out to be a rainy day. Confederate cavalry spotted Union wagons and ambulances going toward Fredericksburg. General Lee thought that the Union was leaving Spotsylvania. General Lee decided to move his artillery out of the "Mule Shoe" before the rain got heavy and the roads turned to mud. Before the artillery got too far down the road, they realized the Yankees were not pulling out. They then returned to their positions by early the next morning.

On May 12 at 4:30 a.m., 15,000 men of the Union Second Corps under General Winfield Scott Hancock charged, Upton-style, with fixed bayonets, going across a field and through a fog of misty, light rain toward Edward Landrum's farm. They caught some of the Confederates returning their cannons to their former positions. About twenty cannons were captured without firing a shot. When the rest of the infantry tried to fire their weapons, their powder was damp from the weather and would not fire. The Union ended up taking over 3,000 prisoners. The Confederates did set into motion more counterattacks that stalled the Union attacks.

May 12 and 13 combined were the deadliest days of the battle. There was a section where the "Mule Shoe" was weak at the end in a slight curve. The fighting there was so bad it picked up the name "Bloody Angle." A ravine was directly in front of the Confederate defense there, which offered protection for thousands of attacking Yankee soldiers.

From 6:00 a.m. on May 12 until 3:00 a.m. May 13 fighting was terrible, it was mostly hand-to-hand combat. People were shot and stabbed through the crevices and the holes between the logs and rocks. Men would be in a position to kill and would hold that position, while others gave them loaded weapons, over and over until they were killed. They would find a hole or crevices where they could stab a man when he stopped or walked by. Then a man would reach the top of the wall and have men feeding him weapons to shoot men until he was shot. A Mississippian stated that in the Confederate trenches, the dead were found piled up five bodies high. Some of the wounded on the bottom were drowned in blood.

From May 14 until May 19 fighting continued near Spotsylvania. The Union continued to attack the Confederate position south of Spotsylvania Court House and were attacked by Confederate cavalry. This delayed the Union long enough for the Confederates to reinforce their infantry and meet the Union threat at Myers Hill. Fighting continued for days with battles here and there, armies pushing and shoving against one another. On May 18, Union forces under the command of General Winfield Scott Hancock and Horatio G. Write attacked General Robert E. Lee's defensive line at Harrison Field near the courthouse. Remnants of General Richard S. Ewell's Corps put a stop to the Union attack.

On May 19, 1864, at the Battle of Harris Farm near Spotsylvania Court House, the Confederates under General Richard S. Ewell attacked the Union troops. These men were fresh troops that had just come in from Washington, D.C. General Ewell loses nine hundred men in that day's fight.

As night fell Grant broke off fighting and sent certain elements of his army to the east, hoping that General Lee would follow. General Lee did not follow but chased Grant south to North Anna River, where General Grant caught up with General Lee. They fought for two days, May 27 and 28, along the banks of the North Anna River. Their next battle would be at Cold Harbor. After two days of fighting with no results for either side, here at Totopotomoy Creek just northeast of Richmond, Lt. General Ulysses S. Grant And General Robert E. Lee turned their attention toward the crossroads of Cold Harbor.

Cold Harbor
May 31-June 12, 1864

On May 31, 1864, Major General Philip Sheridan's cavalry captured Cold Harbor. The next day General Sheridan had to hold the crossroads against the attacks of the Confederacy. General Grant also set out an attack with two of his corps on June 1. The Union gained ground, and two days later General Grant set out another attack. Before dawn Grant attacked with elements of five Union corps. The Confederates were well dug in and ready for their attack. When the Union attacked they were massacred by Lee's infantry. Both sides remained in place, not able to move the other. Finally, General Grant decided to pull out and go to the Confederate rail center of Petersburg, ending the Battle of Cold Harbor on June 12, 1864.

Cold Harbor

Total Forces

170,000

Casualties

17,332

Union	Confederate
12,737	4,595

Killed

1,844	83

Wounded

9,077	3,380

Missing/Captured

1,816	1,132

Siege Of Petersburg
June 15-April 2, 1865

The Siege of Petersburg lasted nine months, two weeks, and two days. General Ulysses S. Grant constructed trenches that extended over thirty miles from the outskirts of Richmond to the outskirts of Petersburg.

Eventually, General Lee, under the pressure of the losses he was suffering in the fighting, retreated to Appomattox Court House.

During the siege, there was fighting almost every day with only a few days where there was no fighting at all. Casualties were mounting on both sides with no end in sight. This was not a fight until one gave up but a fight to the death.

The Union wanted to take control of the three main railroads running in and out of Petersburg or destroy them if necessary. They spent much time destroying railroad tracks up to as much as thirty miles at a time.

This crippled transportation to major cities and took the

Confederacy several weeks to repair tracks. Then the Union started destroying the train engines and cars, burning them. This was having a terrible effect on the morale of the Confederate soldiers, and General Lee was having problems with illnesses, wounded soldiers, no supplies, few officers, and desertion. Men were deserting hundreds at a time and going home, giving up on the War.

On September 5, 1865, General Rooney Lee had an element of his division go behind enemy lines and with light resistance, stole 2,486 beef cattle from the Yankees. By 8:00 a.m., they had driven the cattle back to Confederate lines and were soon back to Petersburg. That evening the Confederate soldiers had a well-deserved feast. A visitor to General Grant's headquarters asked the General, "When do you expect to starve out Lee and capture Richmond?" Grant said, "Never if our armies continue to supply him with beef cattle."

The Union, in late June, started digging a tunnel with a "T" at the end. It was 511 feet long, and the end extended 75 feet in each direction. It was filled with 8000 pounds of gun powder, then buried 20 feet under the Confederate lines. At 4:44 a.m. on July 30 the explosives were set off, instantly killing between 250 and 300 Confederate soldiers.

The Union soldiers charged into the crater instead of going around the top. They had no ladders to get out and were shot down with few surviving. That crater still exists today.

General Lee had many men that were sick and wounded. They were low on supplies, and he had lost contact with most of his officers. General Grant had taken control of all the railroads and blocked General

Lee's supply line to his troops. Richmond had been captured, so on the night of April 2, 1865, under the cover of darkness General Lee divided his forces and went toward Appomattox, Virginia.

Siege Of Petersburg

Strength

Union	Confederate
125,000	60,000

Casualties/losses

42,000	28,000

Desertion

25,000

Appomattox Court House
April 9, 1865

At dawn on April 9, 1865, the Confederate Second Corps under Major General John B. Gordon attacked Sheridan's cavalry and quickly forced back his first line. General Gordon's troops charged through the Union lines and took the ridge. As they took the ridge they saw the entire Union XXIV Corps in line for battle. Lee's cavalry saw the Union forces, withdrew, and rode toward Lynchburg to meet a supply train. General Ord's Union troops began to advance against Gordon's corps while the Union II Corps began to move against General James Longstreet's corps.

General Gordon sent General Lee a message and said that his men were completely given out and were not able to put up a fight anymore. When General Lee heard this he said there was nothing left to do but the inevitable: "Then there is nothing left for me to do but to go and see General Grant, and I would rather die a thousand deaths." General Lee asked for a suspension of fighting while he sought to learn the terms of surrender from General Grant. A white linen dishcloth was used as a truce flag for the Confederacy as one of General Longstreet's staff officers was met and delivered the message into the line of General Custer. General Custer was led back to meet General Longstreet. General Custer said, "In the name of General Sheridan, I demand the unconditional surrender of this army." Longstreet replied that he was not in command of this army, but if he were he would not deal with messages from Sheridan.

At 8:00 a.m. General Lee rode out to meet General Grant, with some of his aides. When General Grant received the letter his migraine headache went away. He handed the letter to his assistant to read to him. In his reply, he revealed where he was located at the time and gave General Lee the right to chose the location for the meeting.

General Lee sent an aide, Charles Marshall, to find a suitable location. He chose a small village of about twenty buildings that served as a way-station for travelers. He selected the home of Wilmer McLean who had lived near Manassas Junction during the First Battle of Bull Run. McLean chose to get away from the war and went to Appomattox, Virginia. A cease-fire was set in place right away and the word was spread that the War was coming to an end.

General Lee arrived at Wilmer McLean's home before general Grant. He was wearing his ceremonial white uniform. When General Grant arrived he was wearing a mud-spattered uniform, a sack coat, and trousers tucked into muddy boots with no sidearms and his tarnished shoulder straps showing his rank. It was the first time the two men had met in twenty years.

The final agreement was that the Confederate soldiers would be put on parole, give up their arms, and return home. The officers were allowed to keep their sidearms, horses, and personal baggage. The defeated soldiers were to take their horses and mules to carry out spring planting and supply Lee's army with food.

Terms of the surrender were recorded, handwritten by General Grant's adjutant, Ely S. Parker, a Native American of the Seneca Tribe, and completed around 4:00 p.m. April 9, 1865.

MARTY STANDISH WAR ENDS

CHAPTER ELEVEN
April 12, 1861-May 9, 1865

At 4:00 p.m. on April 9, 1865, the terms of surrender were recorded at the home of Wilmer McLean between General Robert E. Lee of the Confederate States of America and General Ulysses S. Grant of the Union Army of the United States of America. This, for the most part, put an end to the War between the States of America although there would be those who would hold out until the very end.

Major Marty Standish was one of those who fought at the Battle of Appomattox Court House on that great day in April 1865. On that day the War did end for him, and as an officer, he was granted his sidearms and his horse. With a supply of food, he rode off for home.

As Marty rode home, he was troubled over the many ventures he had to go through during the war. There were many hardships and pains with the loss of many friends he had made over the four years. He realized he had changed and not for the better but in a lot of ways for the worse. Could he ever live a normal life or ever get a normal night's sleep again without thinking of the killing and torture that was done during the war and when he could have stopped and not continued. How many times did he feel that he went too far?

This was something that he may never get over. Would God Jehovah ever find in his heart to forgive people for what they did in the war? These were a lot of burdens for a man to carry for the rest of his life, but hopefully, he would someday be able to forget most of it. Marty is thinking to himself, One thing is for sure, as for me I don't want to ever speak of my experiences again to anyone. I may one day, if the need were ever to arise, write it down for some reason but that would be a serious reason.

As he rides along the meadows of green grass and cool breeze, Marty Standish's thoughts wander off to those of his father and mother sitting on the porch. How they held hands and would lean over and tenderly kiss one another. Then they would later get up to go in the house as his father would open the screen door for his mother to go in. Those thoughts were good and made him impatient to get home, but home was a long, long way off.

He rode until it was about dusk and started looking for a good place to bed down for the night. He came to the top of a hill with a clearing and a large oak tree. He decided he would bed there for the night; it was a full moon and a clear night. Maybe he could get a good night's sleep. He had trouble getting to sleep, fearing the enemy would invade his camp. He just couldn't get used to the idea that the war was over.

He finally did get to sleep for about an hour, then got up, walked around, and checked the horse and gear. Sitting next to the tree and staring out across the valley below, he again thought about past battles the battles that he came close to dying in and how his loyal men came to his rescue, putting their lives in danger. He was so glad that he decided to train his men in the tactics of hand-to-hand combat. That made his men a first-rate guerrilla war, fighting team who were the best in their division, and even larger than that, they were the most decorated in their division.

Yes, Major Standish was coming home a war hero, but there would be no home parades or community picnic, just a family dinner. One thing that history has proven is that the winner of any war decides the outcome of everything: the winner of battles, the number of causalities, the heroes, and how history records it.

After a couple of hours, Marty got tired, lay down, and went to sleep, getting up just before sunrise. He built a fire and made breakfast, then was on the road again. The day was beginning to get cloudy and look like rain. As midday got nearer, it began to rain a little mist, just enough to have a man get out his rain gear. As the rain picked up, it burst into a rainstorm. He was looking for a good place to stop and get out of the rain when he saw a farmhouse off the road. He rode down, got off his horse, and knocked on the door. A young woman answered. Marty asked if he could come in out of the rain. The lady said yes; she said her family had just finished lunch, and he was welcome to eat.

Marty said he was traveling through, got caught in the rainstorm, and was looking for shelter when he spotted their house. She said the rest of the family had gone to the barn to do the spring planting. They may change their minds and come back to the house if this storm does not let up. They talked about the war and how good it was that it was finally over. She said she lost two brothers in the war, one at the Second Battle of Bull Run and the other at Cold Harbor.

Finally the storm passed, and Marty went on his way. He

thanked the young lady and headed out. As he traveled down the road he couldn't help but think about how beautiful the young woman was. He only wished he had a woman like that to come home to. Now, that would really be something to think about. Then he realized, if he had that to keep him occupied during the war, he may not have come home alive.

The weather had cleared, and he continued on his way toward Goshen Swamp, North Carolina. A place only a handful of people in the world knew about. Yet, to Marty, it was the Garden of Eden and the best place in the world to live. Marty didn't know it, but he had changed so much that the garden was not going to settle him down. The war had changed him, and he had to leave and find himself. He would find out that would not be easy for him.

Marty continued on the road toward home. The closer he got to home the poorer the conditions were for the people.

People were starving, and their homes were burned out; towns were destroyed. It would take a lot of money from the north to restore the south and a lot of time. There would be a lot of people who would get rich off the poor with this restoration.

This was the time for a smart man to get established in a legitimate business if he worked his cards right. Jay Standish thought about this, but he just was not settled down enough to think seriously about it.

Marty had just entered the flatlands of North Carolina. Times were still hard here but not as bad as further north. The farms were working, but not much was growing, mostly being planted for the spring. People were still low on food and other supplies. It was good that the Northern army supplied him well before he set out for home. He found a nice clean dry spot at the edge of the forest to sleep for the night. About 2:00 a.m. he heard his horse getting excited like he was scared. He quietly raised to his knees, getting his pistol and crawling closer to his horse. Suddenly a medium size bear tried to attack his horse. Marty shot the bear four times, killing it. He spent the rest of the morning skinning it and cutting up the meat.

He loaded up after breakfast and headed on his way. He came upon a farmhouse late in the afternoon and decided to see if they might let him spend the night. As it turned out, there were three women in their thirties at the house. Their husbands were brothers and owned the farm. They hadn't come home from the war, and the women hadn't eaten in days. They were living on raw corn from the field until now. He asked if they had any salt. They said yes, there was plenty in the smokehouse. He went out and got them the bear meat, but first gave them a can each of beans. This would hold them until he could cook them a little of the bear meat. He made them coffee and went out to the smokehouse to get some salt. After he salted the rest of the bear meat for them so it would not spoil, they all talked for a spell and went to sleep.

Before sunrise, Marty rose, packed, and left without saying goodbye. It made him feel good that he was able to give the bear meat to someone in such need. If he had kept it, most of it would have gone bad before he could have eaten it without salt to preserve it. When he left the farm, he took some of the salt for himself, as salt is hard to come by.

Marty was amazed at how well his journey had been going so far. He had not run into any robbers or thieves yet, and that was unusual. He decided that from here on in he would pay closer attention to his surroundings and the people he met.

A couple of days went by and he went through a small community. It had a lot of small houses that were burned out, and the people were living outside. When he rode through he noticed he got the attention of a couple of men standing next to a fire barrel. As he rode out, he noticed that they had mounted their horses and followed him. He rode out for about an hour until about dusk. He stopped at a tiny clearing at the edge of the woods and tied his horse, taking off his saddle as the men rode by. He built a fire, then he made his bedroll as if he was sleeping in it with his boots next to it and his hat over the head. He stepped back into the edge of the woods and waited. He didn't have to wait long. The men came back, firing into the bedroll.

Thinking they had killed him, he opened fire killing both men at the same time with no mercy, just as they had shown.

Marty left the men where they had fallen, gathered his bedroll, saddled his horse, and went on his way into the night. He went far enough down the road that he found a suitable place to bed for the night off the road. The next morning he got up early and went on his way. A few more days and he would be going through Goldsboro, North Carolina. He would then be around twenty-five miles from the entrance of Goshen Swamp and close to home. He was now getting excited. The days were getting longer. He would be home before he knew it.

After many days, Marty arrived in Mount Olive, North Carolina. He stopped by the railroad depot, and they still remembered him and his brother and the other men. A few of the other men, three they said, had made it home already. They said the people at the supply store would like to see him before he left. Marty said, "For sure."

He had to pick up some extra supplies anyway. After going by and picking up his supplies, he headed toward home after four long hard years.

He wanted to see who the other men were that made it home, hoping one would be Jay, his brother. This ride was a lonely seventeen miles to the entrance of the swamp. He was not sure if he remembered how to get to the camp or not, but he was sure there would be a scout on watch that would.

When Marty got to the entrance, he didn't have to ride his horse far into the swamp before the scout spotted him. He quickly came out of the trees and greeted Marty. They took the horse and boat and headed toward the camp. Marty said he was worried the horse might not make it to camp. The scout said he felt that it could and if not, they would let him loose to roam in the swamp. He would soon find grass and vegetation like the deer.

After six weeks Marty was home to greet his mother and father and two younger brothers his father and mother had while they were at war. His mother said she still wanted a girl; they were starting a second family. As Marty turned around, Jay grabbed him and hugged the breath out of him. It was so good for the two to be with the family again.

Jay told Marty he had something important to tell him, and it needed to be moved on as soon as possible, "Tomorrow is best" he urged. "Please, talk with me tonight; we need to get the men together and be ready to go at daylight."

Jay had been able to get his horse to the camp also. So they had two horses to take with them when they left. They would need the three wagons from the farmer if he still had them. A man was sent that day to tell the farmer when they needed the wagons and horses.

Jay explained that men from his cavalry attacked a platoon of around thirty- five Yankees who had stolen 2,500 tons of gold from the Confederacy outside Charlotte, N.C., They killed all thirty-five Yankees but lost twenty-five of his men. The ten men he had left were taking the gold toward Springville, N.C. when one of the wagons started to break down.

"We took the gold and hid it in a little washed-out cave in the side of a cleft, next to a large red oak tree, covering the entrance with a large stone," Jay said. "Then we took the wagons about a hundred miles away from the location of the gold. I know the area well, but I don't know about the others. If they know, it won't be long before they try to recover it. That is why we need to get started as soon as we can."

They selected their men and went to bed to get a good night's rest. Early the next morning, everyone was on the move and heading to the farmer's house. He had two large farm wagons and a small one with two horses for each wagon. Each wagon had two men and there were Marty and Jay on horseback. It would take them the best part of the day to get to Springville, N.C. if they didn't have trouble running into the Union cavalry.

Coming back they would need some way to camouflage the gold in the wagons. There was too much gold to build false bottoms in the wagons. They would need to do some thinking on that. Marty brought a lot of money with him in case they had to buy someone off. As they were traveling across the farm country, he noticed a farm with a couple of grain silos in the yard. He told Jay, "Maybe we can buy some grain, fill the wagons, and put the gold into the wagons with the grain. Let's hope he has some grain!"

They pulled up to the farmhouse and Marty went to the door and knocked. It was late in the afternoon, and the farmer was eating supper. Marty told him he wanted to buy grain: wheat, corn, oats, whatever he had. The man said he had some wheat and corn he would let go of but not until morning. He said they could all bed down there in the yard and build themselves some fires.

The next morning, they were up early and ready to go when the farmer came out. He filled the two large wagons with wheat and the small wagon with corn. They were able to pay the man his price and go on their way. Before lunch, maybe in an hour or so, they will be at the location of the gold. It was well out of the way from everything, and when they removed the rock and crawledinside, they found the gold, just where Jay had left it.

So they started making room in the wagons on the bottom for the gold, evenly spacing the load to balance the weight, making it easier for the horses to pull it.

The men worked fast, and before long, the wagons were ready to go. It was good they had strong farm wagons for the bulk of the load. Small wagons like the other one they had would never have made the trip with the heavy loads. They would stop for the night in about five hours and be home tomorrow. It would take much longer to unload the gold. They would decide when they got home how much grain they needed. If any is left, they will give it to the farmer when they take the wagons back.

They stopped for the night and got a good night's rest.

Starting early the next morning, they reached Mount Olive and stopped at the hardware store and trading post and gave them a good supply of grain each at no charge. They know the favor will come back to them in good time. They told them that theyknew the people were facing hard times after the war and they wanted to help.

Then the men headed home. When they got to the swamp, there were the boats. They had others bring a few extra boats to help carry the load. They were able to load most of the gold on the boats, but there was a lot they had to bury until they could come back for more. It would take about three months, and the farmer would need his horses and wagons before then.

They decided to take the wagons and horses to the farmer and if he needed the wagons, to unload them in his barn and use them. If not, leave them loaded and use as much grain as he needed. They would be back in about six weeks and tell him what they would do with the grain.

In no time, they had gotten the gold moved to the camp and divided up between the 129 family heads. That gave each family head just a little less than 40 pounds of gold each for a total of $1,290,000 worth of gold.

The price of gold an ounce in 1865 was $15.44 an ounce and in 2021 it was $1,816.17 an ounce. Those figures would run a small calculator off the charts. Today it would be worth searching for that lost pirate camp in Goshen Swamp.

A year later, around April 21, 1866, Marty and Jay are both having a hard time settling down. They spend most of their time in the swamp or getting drunk. When they sleep, they have violent nightmares and are up pacing the floor or going outside walking in the dark. These men, like the others that came back, are damaged goods that can't be repaired. Jay tells Marty he is going to the mountains somewhere that man has not inhabited yet where he can be alone and live in the wild.

Early the next morning, Jay Standish was packed in one of the boats and with his horse, said goodbye to his family. He headed out toward the mountains of Montana … to what he had no idea. He just knew he had to go! Go somewhere, be on the move, he could not stay in one place for very long. That, for some reason now, was against his nature.

He stopped in Mount Olive and found a pack mule he could take with him to carry his supplies. He went to the supply store and the trading post to get enough supplies for most of the trip. Then he headed out.

About mid-summer, Jay Standish had reached the foothills of the mountains in Montana. He stopped at a small town called Woodstock. There he got some supplies and information about where the best places were to trap where the rivers and streams would be plentiful. When he found where he should go, a place that was uninhabited by humans, he set out.

Jay was excited about the adventure that lay ahead for him. He had never set out on his own like this before in his life. The war was long gone and forgotten. He was at peace with himself and pleased with the decision he had made. The one problem the people said he would have was the Indians; they were the Blackfoot. They were not friendly people, and he was warned to make sure that he never showed any sign of fear. They respect someone who shows that he is a brave man, especially in battle.

Jay spent several weeks traveling through the mountains, looking for a good spot to build a cabin for the winter. Time was running out, but finally, he found a valley with a good stream of fresh, clear water. It had a grassy flat spot to build his cabin on up from the stream, with many trees growing around it. It was late in the afternoon when he found the spot, and he decided to make camp. The next morning he got up before sunrise, built his fire, and ate a healthy breakfast.

Starting early, he began cutting down several trees and stacking them in a pile. Then he set stones flush as he could get with the ground, making them level for his foundation. Then he started building his cabin. Using his horse and the mule was a great aid in building the cabin. In two months he had built the cabin and a double stall for cover for the horse and mule.

Finally, he was living in his home in the mountains with a warm fire to comfort him, but his food was getting low, and winter was just around the corner. The next morning he would take his horse and mule and go hunting for deer, bear, or whatever he could find. He would set several traps along the stream if he could find a beaver dam. He didn't travel far up the stream before he came upon a beaver dam. He wasted no time setting the traps; he wanted to get started on the hunting trip as quickly as he could. Jay traveled just inside the tree line of the woods where the animals coming down for water could not see him. There were a lot of wolves traveling around in packs looking for prey.

At this point, it was midday, and he had seen a lot of tracks, yet no game. He felt confident with all the tracks he had seen that there were several different large game animals around. He was tracking a good size herd of deer that looked promising. The trail was so clear that he was able to travel faster, making up much time. He finally reached the crest of a hill with trees, and on the other side, in the valley, he saw a herd of around eighteen deer grazing on the grass. He selected the largest buck in the herd, and with one shot, he fell to the ground. The rest of the herd fled in fear into the woods.

Captain J. Standish then rode down, took the buck, and loaded it on the mule. Then he headed back to the cabin. When he got back, it was getting dark, but he still had to dress out the buck. He had built a hanger for skinning his kills, so he hung the buck to skin. After cutting the meat out, he dressed it in salt to preserve the meat. Then he went inside to make himself coffee and a good meal for supper. Then he went to bed; he would finish skinning and treating the skin tomorrow. The next morning he did do the skin and stretched it out to dry. He went back to the cabin and hung the meat inside at the back of his cabin, out of his way.

He still needed more meat to get through the winter. So he went out to check his traps. He had trapped two large beavers, which is not bad at all.

The winter was not as bad as he had expected except for the cold. He almost froze to death because he did not have enough firewood. The winter in Montana is different than in North Carolina. About 60 degrees different… colder. The Captain decided that come spring he would kill at least two large bears for bed covering. If he couldn't, he would spend the next winter in

North Carolina. He was not going through another winter like the last one again in his life if he had any control over it.

He said he had heard of a snow blizzard before and thought one time he was in one, but he found out last winter that he had never been in one. Next year there would be a lot of firewood cut in time for winter, and it would be piled real close to the cabin. There would be a lot stored inside the cabin for the blizzards when they came so he would not have to go outside. If you went outside during the blizzard, your lungs would freeze if you were not covered VERY well.

Monday, March 30, 1868, is windy and cold in the mountains, with a lot of snow still on the ground. Everything is alive in the warm sun, and getting ready to produce young for the new spring to come. The mother of fertility, springtime, has arrived for all creation under the sun: all life, plants, animals, trees, wildlife, and mankind. What a blessing.

Captain Standish feels that if he is to kill a large bear he has to go deeper into the woods, in the mountains. He travels many days and sees signs of bears clawing on the trees. He continues to follow the signs, and then he hears men shouting and the growling of a bear. He ties his horse and mule to a small tree. Taking his gun and pistol, he goes quietly toward the sounds. As he lies quietly hidden, he watches as four Indians have cornered a large bear in a gully. Their arrows and spears are missing and are not hitting vital organs. They are just making the bear more vicious, and he charges the men, tearing them from limb to limb, throwing them to the ground, and doing his best to kill them.

The Captain sees that the Indians are in real trouble and are about to be killed and fires a shot at the bear with his gun. Then the bear charges the Captain. He doesn't have time to reload his gun, so he pulls his pistol and fires quickly at the bear, but by then the bear is on him. He takes his knife, stabbing the bear as he falls dead to the ground lying on top of the Captain.

The Captain is not seriously harmed and pushes the bear off of him, getting to his feet. Then he goes to the Indians and finds two dead and two badly wounded. He takes the two that are wounded and treats their wounds the best he knows how. He has had a little medical training from college but only enough to help in a bad situation. Maybe that will be enough to save these men.

The Captain spends over a week, feeding and treating the Indians. They can move around a little now, but communication is little to none. The youngest one, before he passed out, saw the Captain kill the bear and save their lives. He did figure out that much. The Captain had a lot of bear meat for them to eat before they set out to travel. He had skinned the bear for the winter already. Early the next morning, they set out to travel home, but the Indians wanted the Captain to come and meet their Chief. He decided he would go because it might be good in the long run.

After a day and a half journey, they came to a very large Indian village next to a river. In the center of the village was the chief's teepee. When they arrived, the chief, with his headband of eagle feathers, came out and gladly grabbed the two Indians. Hugging them with all his might and kissing them on the cheeks, he was overjoyed to see them.

Then they spoke to him about the Captain who just stood there straight and solid without smiling. The Chief invited the two Indians and the Captain into his teepee, for a smoke of his pipe. Then they told him what had happened. The Chief was well impressed with the Captain's bravery and helping his braves. As it turned out, the young brave was his only son and the other brave was his only brother.

The Chief had a teepee set up for Captain Standish in their camp, so he could come and go as he pleased. He was always welcome and had his choice of any squaw for a wife if he chose, even the Chief's daughter, who was outstandingly beautiful. The Captain told the Chief that if he chose a wife, it would be his daughter but only if that was her choice.

They wanted him to stay and learn their language, and teach them his. He said he would stay until it was time for him to get ready for winter; then he must go. The Chief said his daughter and his son would teach him the language of the Blackfoot and he would teach them the White Man language.

The Captain learned fast; it was just another language to him. The Blackfoot also learned fast. The Chief's son was named Kitchi, meaning brave, and his sister's name was Nadie, meaning wise. The Chief's brother's name was Achak, meaning spirit. The Chief's name was Chief Crow Foot, and he had lived many years and was a friend to the white man.

As time went by, Captain J. Standish went back and forth from his cabin to the Blackfoot tribe and finally married the Indian princess, Nadie. They had several children and made the Chief a very happy man.

Jay Standish wrote his brother Marty letters about his adventures and convinced him to do the same. Marty Standish chose to head out toward Oregon and see the big country out there.

This is not the end of the stories of gold, the Standishes, and Goshen Swamp. There is more to be told in the coming days. The camp at Goshen Swamp will be hit with a bad case of malaria.